Chadwick was sitting behind his desk.

Serena knew she shouldn't think of him as Chadwick—it was too familiar. Too personal. Mr. Beaumont was her boss. She worked hard for him, pulling long hours whenever necessary.

It wasn't a secret that Serena would go to the ends of the earth for this man. It *was* a secret that she'd always done just a little more than admire his commitment to the company.

Chadwick Beaumont was an incredibly handsome man—a solid six-two, his sandy-blond hair neatly trimmed at all times. He would be one of those men who aged like a fine wine, only getting better with each passing year. Some days, Serena would catch herself staring as if she were trying to savor him.

But that secret admiration was buried deep.

She had an excellent job with benefits and she would never risk it by doing something as unprofessional as falling in love with her boss. They worked together. Their relationship was nothing but business-professional.

She had no idea how being pregnant was going to change things.

* * *

Not the Boss's Baby is part of The Beaumont Heirs series: One Colorado family, limitless scandal!

* * *

If you're on Twitter,
tell us what you think of Harlequin Desire!
#harlequindesire

Dear Reader,

I'm proud to introduce The Beaumont Heirs—a brand-new series set in Colorado. The Beaumonts are one of Denver's oldest, most preeminent families. They're also owners of the Beaumont Brewery, founded by Phillipe Beaumont back in the 1880s. The Beaumont Brewery is world-famous for the team of Percherons that pulls the Beaumont wagon in commercials and parades.

The Beaumont heirs are the children of Hardwick Beaumont, the third-generation Beaumont to run the Brewery. Although he's been dead for almost a decade, Hardwick's womanizing ways—the four marriages and divorces, the ten children and uncounted illegitimate children—are still leaving ripples in the Beaumont family.

Chadwick Beaumont is the oldest Beaumont heir. He was Hardwick's chosen successor. His father expected perfection from his oldest child and Chadwick has spent his whole life trying to do as his father wished. But as his siblings run through the family fortune and the Brewery is subject to a hostile takeover bid, Chadwick finds himself wondering what he's really been working for all these years.

And when his executive assistant, Ms. Serena Chase, reveals she's pregnant—and quite single—Chadwick realizes what he's wanted for years. *Her*.

Not the Boss's Baby is a sensual story about discovering what you want and falling in love. I hope you enjoy reading this book as much as I enjoyed writing it! For more information about the other Beaumont heirs, be sure to stop by www.sarahmanderson.com!

Sarah

NOT THE BOSS'S BABY

—

SARAH M. ANDERSON

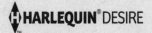

Recycling programs
for this product may
not exist in your area.

ISBN-13: 978-0-373-73341-5

NOT THE BOSS'S BABY

Printed in U.S.A.

Books by Sarah M. Anderson

Harlequin Desire

A Man of His Word #2130
A Man of Privilege #2171
A Man of Distinction #2184
A Real Cowboy #2211
Straddling the Line #2232
Bringing Home the Bachelor #2254
Expecting a Bolton Baby #2267
What a Rancher Wants #2282
‡*Not the Boss's Baby* #2328

*The Bolton Brothers
‡The Beaumont Heirs

Other titles by this author available in ebook format.

SARAH M. ANDERSON

Award-winning author Sarah M. Anderson may live east of the Mississippi River, but her heart lies out west on the Great Plains. With a lifelong love of horses and two history teachers for parents, she had plenty of encouragement to learn everything she could about the tribes of the Great Plains.

When she started writing, it wasn't long before her characters found themselves out in South Dakota among the Lakota Sioux. She loves to put people from two different worlds into new situations and to see how their backgrounds and cultures take them someplace they never thought they'd go.

Sarah's book *A Man of Privilege* won the 2012 RT Reviewers' Choice Award for Best Harlequin Desire.

When not helping out at her son's school or walking her rescue dogs, Sarah spends her days having conversations with imaginary cowboys and American Indians, all of which is surprisingly well-tolerated by her wonderful husband. Readers can find out more about Sarah's love of cowboys and Indians at www.sarahmanderson.com.

To Leah Hanlin. We've been friends for over twenty years now, and I'm so glad I've been able to share this journey—and my covers!—with you. Let's celebrate by getting more sleep!

One

"Ms. Chase, if you could join me in my office."

Serena startled at the sound of Mr. Beaumont's voice coming from the old-fashioned intercom on her desk. Blinking, she became aware of her surroundings.

How on earth had she gotten to work? She looked down—she was wearing a suit, though she had no memory of getting dressed. She touched her hair. All appeared to be normal. Everything was fine.

Except she was pregnant. Nothing fine or normal about *that*.

She was relatively sure it was Monday. She looked at the clock on her computer. Yes, nine in the morning—the normal time for her morning meeting with Chadwick Beaumont, President and CEO of the Beaumont Brewery. She'd been Mr. Beaumont's executive assistant for seven years now, after a yearlong internship and a year working in Human Resources. She could count the number of times they'd missed their 9:00 a.m. Monday meeting on two hands.

No need to let something like a little accidental pregnancy interrupt that.

Okay, so everything had turned upside down this past weekend. She wasn't just a little tired or a tad stressed out. She wasn't fighting off a bug, even. She was, in all likelihood, two months and two or three weeks pregnant. She knew that with certainty because those were the last times she'd slept with Neil.

Neil. She had to tell him she was expecting. He had a right to know. God, she didn't want to see him again— to be rejected again. But this went way beyond what she wanted. What a huge mess.

"Ms. Chase? Is there a problem?" Mr. Beaumont's voice was strict but not harsh.

She clicked the intercom on. "No, Mr. Beaumont. Just a slight delay. I'll be right in."

She was at work. She had a job to do—a job she needed now more than ever.

Serena sent a short note to Neil informing him that she needed to talk to him, and then she gathered up her tablet and opened the door to Chadwick Beaumont's office. Chadwick was the fourth Beaumont to run the brewery, and it showed in his office. The room looked much as it might have back in the early 1940s, soon after Prohibition had ended, when Chadwick's grandfather John had built it. The walls were mahogany panels that had been oiled until they gleamed. A built-in bar with a huge mirror took up the whole interior wall. The exterior wall was lined with windows hung with heavy gray velvet drapes and crowned with elaborately hand-carved woodwork that told the story of the Beaumont Brewery.

The conference table had been custom-made to fit the

room—Serena had read that it was so large and so heavy that John Beaumont had to have the whole thing built in the office because there was no getting it through a doorway. Tucked in the far corner by a large coffee table was a grouping of two leather club chairs and a matching leather loveseat set. The coffee table was supposedly made of one of the original wagon wheels that Phillipe Beaumont had used when he'd crossed the Great Plains with a team of Percheron draft horses back in the 1880s on his way to settle in Denver and make beer.

Serena loved this room—the opulence, the history. Things she didn't have in her own life. The only changes that reflected the twenty-first century were a large flatscreen television that hung over the sitting area and the electronics on the desk, which had been made to match the conference table. A door on the other side of the desk, nearly hidden between the bar and a bookcase, led to a private bathroom. Serena knew that Chadwick had added a treadmill and a few other exercise machines, as well as a shower, to the bathroom, but only because she'd processed the orders. She'd never gone into Chadwick's personal space. Not once in seven years.

This room had always been a source of comfort to her—a counterpoint to the stark poverty that had marked her childhood. It represented everything she wanted—security, stability, *safety*. A goal to strive for. Through hard work, dedication and loyalty, she could have nice things, too. Maybe not this nice, but better than the shelters and rusted-out trailers in which she'd grown up.

Chadwick was sitting behind his desk, his eyes focused on his computer. Serena knew she shouldn't think of him as Chadwick—it was far too familiar. Too personal. Mr. Beaumont was her boss. He'd never made a move on her, never suggested that she "stay late" to work on a project that didn't exist—never booked them on a weekend conference that didn't exist. She worked hard for him, pulling long hours whenever necessary. She did good work for him and he rewarded her. For a girl who'd lived on free school lunches, getting a ten-thousand-dollar bonus *and* an eight-percent-a-year raise, like she had at her last performance review, was a gift from heaven.

It wasn't a secret that Serena would go to the ends of the earth for this man. It *was* a secret that she'd always done just a little more than admire his commitment to the company. Chadwick Beaumont was an incredibly handsome man—a solid six-two, with sandy blond hair that was neatly trimmed at all times. He was probably going gray, but it didn't show with his coloring. He would be one of those men who aged like a fine wine, only getting better with each passing year. Some days, Serena would catch herself staring at him as if she were trying to savor him.

But that secret admiration was buried deep. She had an excellent job with benefits and she would never risk it by doing something as unprofessional as falling in love with her boss. She'd been with Neil for almost ten years. Chadwick had been married as well. They worked together. Their relationship was nothing but business-professional.

She had no idea how being pregnant was going to change things. If she'd needed this job—and health benefits—before, she needed them so much more now.

Serena took her normal seat in one of the two chairs set before Chadwick's desk and powered up her tablet. "Good morning, Mr. Beaumont." Oh, heavens—she'd forgotten to see if she'd put on make-up this morning in her panic-induced haze. At this point, she could only pray she didn't have raccoon eyes.

"Ms. Chase," Chadwick said by way of greeting, his

gaze flicking over her face. He looked back at his monitor, then paused. Serena barely had time to hold her breath before she had Chadwick Beaumont's undivided attention. "Are you okay?"

No. She'd never been less okay in her adult life. The only thing that was keeping her together was the realization that she'd been less okay as a kid and survived. She'd survive this.

She hoped.

So she squared her shoulders and tried to pull off her most pleasant smile. "I'm fine. Monday mornings, you know."

Chadwick's brow creased as he weighed this statement. "Are you sure?"

She didn't like to lie to him. She didn't like to lie to anyone. She had recently had her fill of lying, thanks to Neil. "It'll be fine."

She had to believe that. She'd pulled herself out of sheer poverty by dint of hard work. A bump in the road—a baby bump—wouldn't ruin everything. She hoped.

His hazel eyes refused to let her go for a long moment. But then he silently agreed to let it pass. "Very well, then. What's on tap this week, beyond the regular meetings?"

As always, she smiled at his joke. What was on tap was beer—literally and figuratively. As far as she knew, it was the only joke he ever told.

Chadwick had set appointments with his vice presidents, usually lunch meetings and the like. He was deeply involved in his company—a truly hands-on boss. Serena's job was making sure his irregular appointments didn't mess up his standing ones. "You have an appointment at ten with your lawyers on Tuesday to try and reach a settlement. I've moved your meeting with Matthew to later in the afternoon."

She carefully left out the facts that the lawyers were divorce attorneys and that the settlement was with his soon-to-be-ex-wife, Helen. The divorce had been dragging on for months now—over thirteen, by her count. She did not know the details. Who was to say what went on behind closed doors in any family? All she knew was that the whole process was wearing Chadwick down like waves eroding a beach—slowly but surely.

Chadwick's shoulders slumped a little and he exhaled with more force. "As if this meeting will go any differently than the last five did." But then he added, "What else?" in a forcefully bright tone.

Serena cleared her throat. That was, in a nutshell, the extent of the personal information they shared. "Wednesday at one is the meeting with the Board of Directors at the Hotel Monaco downtown." She cleared her throat. "To discuss the offer from AllBev. Your afternoon meeting with the production managers was cancelled. They're all going to send status reports instead."

Then she realized—she wasn't so much terrified about having a baby. It was the fact that because she was suddenly going to have a baby, there was a very good chance she could lose her job.

AllBev was an international conglomerate that specialized in beer manufacturers. They'd bought companies in England, South Africa and Australia, and now they had their sights set on Beaumont. They were well-known for dismantling the leadership, installing their own skeleton crew of managers, and wringing every last cent of profit out of the remaining workers.

Chadwick groaned and slumped back in his chair. "That's this week?"

"Yes, sir." He shot her a wounded look at the *sir*, so she corrected herself. "Yes, Mr. Beaumont. It got moved up to accommodate Mr. Harper's schedule." In addition to owning one of the largest banks in Colorado, Leon Harper was also one of the board members pushing to accept AllBev's offer.

What if Chadwick agreed or the board overrode his wishes? What if Beaumont Brewery was sold? She'd be out of a job. There was no way AllBev's management would want to keep the former CEO's personal assistant. She'd be shown the door with nothing more than a salvaged copier-paper box of her belongings to symbolize her nine years there.

Maybe that wouldn't be the end of the world—she'd lived as frugally as she could, tucking almost half of each paycheck away in ultra-safe savings accounts and CDs. She couldn't go back on welfare. She *wouldn't*.

If she weren't pregnant, getting another job would be relatively easy. Chadwick would write her a glowing letter of recommendation. She was highly skilled. Even a temp job would be a job until she found another place like Beaumont Brewery.

Except…except for the benefits. She was pregnant. She *needed* affordable health insurance, and the brewery had some of the most generous health insurance around. She hadn't paid more than ten dollars to see a doctor in eight years.

But it was more than just keeping her costs low. She couldn't go back to the way things had been before she'd started working at the Beaumont Brewery. Feeling like her life was out of control again? Having people treat her like she was a lazy, ignorant leech on society again?

Raising a child the way she'd been raised, living on food pantry handouts and whatever Mom could scavenge from her shift at the diner? Of having social workers threaten to take her away from her parents unless they could do better—*be* better? Of knowing she was always somehow less than the other kids at school but not knowing why—until the day when Missy Gurgin walked up to her in fourth grade and announced to the whole class that Serena was wearing the exact shirt, complete with stain, she'd thrown away because it was ruined?

Serena's lungs tried to clamp shut. *No,* she thought, forcing herself to breathe. It wasn't going to happen like that. She had enough to live on for a couple of years— longer if she moved into a smaller apartment and traded down to a cheaper car. Chadwick wouldn't allow the family business to be sold. He would protect the company. He would protect her.

"Harper. That old goat," Chadwick muttered, snapping Serena back to the present. "He's still grinding that ax about my father. The man never heard of letting bygones be bygones, I swear."

This was the first that Serena had heard about this. "Mr. Harper's out to get you?"

Chadwick waved his hand, dismissing the thought. "He's still trying to get even with Hardwick for sleeping with his wife, as the story goes, two days after Harper and his bride got back from their honeymoon." He looked at her again. "Are you sure you're all right? You look pale."

Pale was probably the best she could hope for today. "I…." She grasped at straws and came up with one. "I hadn't heard that story."

"Hardwick Beaumont was a cheating, lying, philandering, sexist bigot on his best day." Chadwick repeated all of this by rote, as if he'd had it beaten into his skull with a dull spoon. "I have no doubt that he did exactly that—or something very close to it. But it was forty years ago. Hardwick's been dead for almost ten years.

Harper...." He sighed, looking out the windows. In the distance, the Rocky Mountains gleamed in the spring sunlight. Snow capped off the mountains, but it hadn't made it down as far as Denver. "I just wish Harper would realize that I'm not Hardwick."

"I know you're not like that."

His eyes met hers. There was something different in them, something she didn't recognize. "Do you? Do you, really?"

This...this felt like dangerous territory.

She didn't know, actually. She had no idea if he was getting a divorce because he'd slept around on his wife. All she knew was that he'd never hit on her, not once. He treated her as an equal. He respected her.

"Yes," she replied, feeling certain. "I do."

The barest hint of a smile curved up one side of his lips. "Ah, that's what I've always admired about you, Serena. You see the very best in people. You make everyone around you better, just by being yourself."

Oh. *Oh.* Her cheeks warmed, although she wasn't sure if it was from the compliment or the way he said her name. He usually stuck to Ms. Chase.

Dangerous territory, indeed.

She needed to change the subject. *Now.* "Saturday night at nine you have the charity ball at the Denver Art Museum."

That didn't erase the half-cocked smile from his face, but it did earn her a raised eyebrow. Suddenly, Chadwick Beaumont looked anything but tired or worn-down. Suddenly, he looked hot. Well, he was always hot—but right now? It wasn't buried beneath layers of responsibility or worry.

Heat flushed Serena's face, but she wasn't entirely sure why one sincere compliment would have been enough to set her all aflutter. Oh, that's right—she was pregnant. Maybe she was just having a hormonal moment.

"What's that for, again? A food bank?"

"Yes, the Rocky Mountain Food Bank. They were this year's chosen charity."

Every year, the Beaumont Brewery made a big splash by investing heavily in a local charity. One of Serena's job responsibilities was personally handling the small mountain of applications that came in every year. A Beaumont Brewery sponsorship was worth about $35 million in related funds and donations—that's why they chose a new charity every year. Most of the non-profits could operate for five to ten years with that kind of money.

Serena went on. "Your brother Matthew planned this event. It's the centerpiece of our fundraising efforts for the food bank. Your attendance will be greatly appreciated." She usually phrased it as a request, but Chadwick had never missed a gala. He understood that this was as much about promoting the Beaumont Brewery name as it was about promoting a charity.

Chadwick still had her in his sights. "You chose this one, didn't you?"

She swallowed. It was almost as if he had realized that the food bank had been an important part of her family's survival—that they would have starved if they hadn't gotten groceries and hot meals on a weekly basis. "Technically, I choose all the charities. It's my job."

"You do it well." But before the second compliment could register, he continued, "Will Neil be accompanying you?"

"Um…." She usually attended these events with Neil. He mostly went to hobnob with movers and shakers, but Serena loved getting all dressed up and drinking champagne. Things she'd never thought possible back when she was a girl.

Things were different now. So, *so* different. Suddenly, Serena's throat closed up on her. God, what a mess.

"No. He…" *Try not to cry, try not to cry.* "We mutually decided to end our relationship several months ago."

Chadwick's eyebrows jumped up so high they almost cleared his forehead. "Several *months* ago? Why didn't you tell me?"

Breathe in, breathe out. Don't forget to repeat.

"Mr. Beaumont, we usually do not discuss our personal lives at the office." It came out pretty well—fairly strong, her voice only cracking slightly over the word *personal.* "I didn't want you to think I couldn't handle myself."

She was his competent, reliable, loyal employee. If she'd told him that Neil had walked out after she'd confronted him about the text messages on his phone and demanded that he recommit to the relationship—by having a baby and finally getting married—well, she'd have been anything but competent. She might be able to manage Chadwick's office, but not her love life.

Chadwick gave her a look that she'd seen before—the one he broke out when he was rejecting a supplier's offer. A look that blended disbelief and disdain into a potent mix. It was a powerful look, one that usually made people throw out another offer—one with better terms for the Brewery.

He'd never looked at her like that before. It bordered on terrifying. He wouldn't fire her for keeping her private life private, would he? But then everything about him softened as he leaned forward in his chair, his elbows on the table. "If this happened several months ago, what happened this weekend?"

"I'm sorry?"

"This weekend. You're obviously upset. I can tell, although you're doing a good job of hiding it. Did he…" Chadwick cleared his throat, his eyes growing hard. "Did he do something to you this weekend?"

"No, not that." Neil might have been a jerk—okay, he *was* a cheating, commitment-phobic jerk—but she couldn't have Chadwick thinking Neil had beaten her. Still, she was afraid to elaborate. Swallowing was suddenly difficult and she was blinking at an unusually fast rate. If she sat there much longer, she was either going to burst into tears or black out. Why couldn't she get her lungs to work?

So she did the only thing she could. She stood and, as calmly and professionally as possible, walked out of the office. Or tried to, anyway. Her hand was on the doorknob when Chadwick said, "Serena, stop."

She couldn't bring herself to turn around and face him—to risk that disdainful look again, or something worse. So she closed her eyes. Which meant that she didn't see him get up or come around his desk, didn't see him walk up behind her. But she heard it—the creaking of his chair as he stood, the footsteps muffled by the thick Oriental rug. The warmth of his body as he stood close to her—much closer than he normally stood.

He placed his hand on her shoulder and turned her. She had no choice but to pivot, but he didn't let go of her. Not entirely. Oh, he released her shoulder, but when she didn't look up at him, he slid a single finger under her chin and raised her face. "Serena, look at me."

She didn't want to. Her face flushed hot from his touch—because that's what he was doing. *Touching* her. His finger slid up and down her chin—if she didn't know better, she'd say he was caressing her. It was the most intimate touch she'd felt in months. Maybe longer.

She opened her eyes. His face was still a respectable foot away from hers—but this was the closest they'd ever been. He could kiss her if he wanted and she wouldn't be able to stop him. She *wouldn't* stop him.

He didn't. This close up, his eyes were such a fine blend of green and brown and flecks of gold. She felt some of her panic fade as she gazed up into his eyes. She was not in love with her boss. Nope. Never had been. Wasn't about to start falling for him now, no matter how he complimented her or touched her. It wasn't going to happen.

He licked his lips as he stared at her. Maybe he was as nervous as she was. This was several steps over a line neither of them had ever crossed.

But maybe…maybe he was hungry. Hungry for her.

"Serena," he said in a low voice that she wasn't sure she'd ever heard him use before. It sent a tingle down her back that turned into a shudder—a shudder he felt. The corner of his mouth curved again. "Whatever the problem is, you can come to me. If he's bothering you, I'll have it taken care of. If you need help or…" She saw his Adam's apple bob as he swallowed. His finger stroked the same square inch of her skin again and she did a whole lot more than shudder. "Whatever you need, it's yours."

She needed to say something here, something professional and competent. But all she could do was look at his lips. What would they taste like? Would he hesitate, waiting for her to take the lead, or would he kiss her as if he'd been dying to do for seven years?

"What do you mean?" She didn't know what she wanted him to say. It *should* sound like an employer expressing concern for the well-being of a trusted em-

ployee—but it didn't. Was he hitting on her after all this
time? Just because Neil was a jerk? Because she was
obviously having a vulnerable moment? Or was there
something else going on there?

The air seemed to thin between them, as if he'd leaned
forward without realizing it. Or perhaps she'd done the
leaning. *He's going to kiss me,* she realized. *He's going
to kiss me and I want him to. I've always wanted him to.*

He didn't. He just ran his finger over her chin again,
as if he were memorizing her every feature. She wanted
to reach up and thread her fingers through his sandy hair,
pull his mouth down to hers. Taste those lips. Feel more
than just his finger.

"Serena, you're my most trusted employee. You always have been. I want you to know that, whatever hap-
pens at the board meeting, I will take care of you. I won't
let them walk you out of this building without anything.
Your loyalty *will* be rewarded. I won't fail you."

All the oxygen she'd been holding in rushed out of
her with a soft "*oh.*"

It was what she needed to hear. God, how she needed
to hear it. She might not have Neil, but all of her hard
work was worth something. She wouldn't have to think
about going back on welfare or declaring bankruptcy or
standing in line at the food pantry.

Then some of her good sense came back to her. This
would be the time to have a business-professional response. "Thank you, Mr. Beaumont."

Something in his grin changed, making him look almost wicked—the very best kind of wicked. "Better than
sir, but still. Call me Chadwick. Mr. Beaumont sounds
too much like my father." When he said this, a hint of
his former weariness crept into his eyes. Suddenly, he
dropped his finger away from her chin and took a step

back. "So, lawyers on Tuesday, Board of Directors on Wednesday, charity ball on Saturday?"

Somehow, Serena managed to nod. They were back on familiar footing now. "Yes." She took another deep breath, feeling calmer.

"I'll pick you up."

So much for that feeling of calm. "Excuse me?"

A little of the wickedness crept back into his smile. "I'm going to the charity gala. You're going to the charity gala. It makes sense that we would go to the charity gala together. I'll pick you up at seven."

"But…the gala starts at nine."

"Obviously we'll go to dinner." She must have looked worried because he took another step back. "Call it…an early celebration for the success of your charity selection this year."

In other words, don't call it a date. Even if that's what it sounded like. "Yes, Mr. Beau—" He shot her a hot look that had her snapping her mouth shut. "Yes, Chadwick."

He grinned an honest-to-God grin that took fifteen years off his face. "There. That wasn't so hard, was it?" Then he turned away from her and headed back to his desk. Whatever moment they'd just had, it was over. "Bob Larsen should be in at ten. Let me know when he gets here."

"Of course." She couldn't bring herself to say his name again. Her head was too busy swimming with everything that had just happened.

She was halfway through the door, already pulling it shut behind her, when he called out, "And Serena? Whatever you need. I mean it."

"Yes, Chadwick."

Then she closed his door.

Two

This was the point in his morning where Chadwick normally reviewed the marketing numbers. Bob Larsen was his handpicked Vice President of Marketing. He'd helped move the company's brand recognition way, way up. Although Bob was closing in on fifty, he had an intrinsic understanding of the internet and social media, and had used it to drag the brewery into the twenty-first century. He'd put Beaumont Brewery on Facebook, then Twitter—never chasing the trend, but leading it. Chadwick wasn't sure exactly what SnappShot did, beyond make pictures look scratched and grainy, but Bob was convinced that it was the platform through which to launch their new line of Percheron Seasonal Ales. "Targeting all those foodies who snap shots of their dinners!" he'd said the week before, in the excited voice of a kid getting a new bike for Christmas.

Yes, that's what Chadwick *should* have been thinking

about. He took his meetings with his department heads seriously. He took the whole company seriously. He rewarded hard work and loyalty and never, ever allowed distractions. He ran a damn tight ship.

So why was he sitting there, thinking about his assistant?

Because he was. Man, was he.

Several months.

Her words kept rattling around in his brain, along with the way she'd looked that morning—drawn, tired. Like a woman who'd cried her eyes out most of the weekend. She hadn't answered his question. If that prick had walked out several months before—and no matter what she said about what 'we decided,' Chadwick had heard the 'he' first—what had happened that weekend?

The thought of Neil Moore—mediocre golf pro always trying to suck up to the next big thing every time Chadwick had met him—doing anything to hurt Serena made him furious. He'd never liked Neil. Too much of a leech, not good enough for the likes of Serena Chase. Chadwick had always been of the opinion that she deserved someone better, someone who wouldn't abandon her at a party to schmooze a local TV personality like he'd witnessed Neil do on at least three separate occasions.

Serena deserved so much better than that ass. Of course, Chadwick had known that for years. Why was it bothering him so much this morning?

She'd looked so…different. Upset, yes, but there was something else going on. Serena had always been unflappable, totally focused on the job. Of course Chadwick had never done anything inappropriate involving her, but he'd caught a few other men assuming she was up for grabs just because she was a woman in Hardwick Beaumont's old office. Chadwick had never done busi-

ness with those men again—which, a few times, meant
going with the higher-priced vendor. It went against the
principles his father, Hardwick, had raised him by—the
bottom line was the most important thing.

Hardwick might have been a lying, cheating bastard,
but that wasn't Chadwick. And Serena knew it. She'd
said so herself.

That had to be why Chadwick had lost his mind and
done something he'd managed not to do for eight years—
touch Serena. Oh, he'd touched her before. She had a hell
of a handshake, one that betrayed no weakness or fear,
something that occasionally undermined other women in
a position of power. But putting his hand on her shoulder?
Running a finger along the sensitive skin under her chin?

Hell.

For a moment, he'd done something he'd wanted to do
for years—engage Serena Chase on a level that went far
beyond his scheduling conflicts. And for that moment,
it'd felt wonderful to see her dark brown eyes look up
at him, her pupils dilating with need—reflecting his desire back at him. To feel her body respond to his touch.

Some days, it felt like he never got to do what he
wanted. Chadwick was the responsible one. The one who
ran the family company and cleaned up the family messes
and paid the family bills while everyone else in the family ran amuck, having affairs and one-night stands and
spending money like it was going out of style.

Just that weekend his brother Phillip had bought some
horse for a million dollars. And what did his little brother
do to pay for it? He went to company-sponsored parties
and drank Beaumont Beer. That was the extent of Phillip's involvement in the company. Phillip always did exactly what he wanted without a single thought for how

it might affect other people—for how it might affect the brewery.

Not Chadwick. He'd been born to run this company. It wasn't a joke—Hardwick Beaumont had called a press conference in the hospital and held the newborn Chadwick up, red-faced and screaming, to proclaim him the future of Beaumont Brewery. Chadwick had the newspaper articles to prove it.

He'd done a good job—so good, in fact, that the Brewery had become the target for takeovers and mergers by conglomerates who didn't give a damn for beer or for the Beaumont name. They just wanted to boost their companies' bottom lines with Beaumont's profits.

Just once, he'd done something he wanted. Not what his father expected or the investors demanded or Wall Street projected—what *he* wanted. Serena had been upset. He'd wanted to comfort her. At heart, it wasn't a bad thing.

But then he'd remembered his father. And that Chadwick seducing his assistant was no better than Hardwick Beaumont seducing his secretary. So he'd stopped. Chadwick Beaumont was responsible, focused, driven, and in no way controlled by his baser animal instincts. He was better than that. He was better than his father.

Chadwick had been faithful while married. Serena had been with—well, he'd never been sure if Neil was her husband, live-in lover, boyfriend, significant other, life partner—whatever people called it these days. Plus, she'd worked for Chadwick. That had always held him back because he was not the apple that had fallen from Hardwick's tree, by God.

All of these correct thoughts did not explain why Chadwick's finger was hovering over the intercom button, ready to call Serena back into the office and ask her again what had happened this weekend. Selfishly, he almost wanted her to break down and cry on his shoulder, just so he could hold her.

Chadwick forced himself to turn back to his monitor and call up the latest figures. Bob had emailed him the analytics Sunday night. Chadwick hated wasting time having something he could easily read explained to him. He was no idiot. Just because he didn't understand *why* anyone would take pictures of their dinner and post them online didn't mean he couldn't see the user habits shifting, just as Bob said they would.

This was better, he thought, as he looked over the numbers. Work. Work was good. It kept him focused. Like telling Serena he was taking her to the gala—a work function. They'd been at galas and banquets like that before. What difference did it make if they arrived in the same car or not? It didn't. It was business related. Nothing personal.

Except it was personal and he knew it. Picking her up in his car, taking her out to dinner? Not business. Even if they discussed business things, it still wouldn't be the same as dinner with, say, Bob Larsen. Serena usually wore a black silk gown with a bit of a fishtail hem and a sweetheart neckline to these things. Chadwick didn't care that it was always the same gown. She looked fabulous in it, a pashmina shawl draped over her otherwise bare shoulders, a small string of pearls resting against her collarbone, her thick brown hair swept up into an artful twist.

No, dinner would not be business-related. Not even close.

He wouldn't push her, he decided. It was the only compromise he could make with himself. He wasn't like his father, who'd had no qualms about making his secretaries' jobs contingent upon sex. He wasn't about to trap Serena into doing anything either of them would regret. He would take her to dinner and then the gala, and would do nothing more than enjoy her company. That was that. He could restrain himself just fine. He'd had years of practice, after all.

Thankfully, the intercom buzzed and Serena's normal, level voice announced that Bob was there. "Send him in," Chadwick replied, thankful to have a distraction from his own thoughts.

He had to fight to keep his company. He had no illusions that the board meeting on Wednesday would go well. He was in danger of becoming the Beaumont who lost the brewery—of failing at the one thing he'd been raised to do.

He did not have time to be distracted by Serena Chase.

And that was final.

The rest of Monday passed without a reply from Neil. Serena was positive about this because she refreshed her email approximately every other minute. Tuesday started much the same. She had her morning meeting with Chadwick where, apart from when he asked her if everything was all right, nothing out of the ordinary happened. No lingering glances, no hot touches and absolutely no near-miss kisses. Chadwick was his regular self, so Serena made sure to be as normal as she could be.

Not to say it wasn't a challenge. Maybe she'd imagined the whole thing. She could blame a lot on hormones now, right? So Chadwick had stepped out of his prescribed role for a moment. She was the one who'd been upset. She must have misunderstood his intent, that's all.

Which left her more depressed than she expected. It's not like she *wanted* Chadwick to make a pass at her. An

intra-office relationship was against company policy—
she knew because she'd helped Chadwick rewrite the
policy when he first hired her. Flings between bosses and
employees set the company up for sexual harassment law-
suits when everything went south—which it usually did.

But that didn't explain why, as she watched him walk
out of the office on his way to meet with the divorce lawyers with his ready-for-battle look firmly in place, she
wished his divorce would be final. Just because the process was draining him, that's all.

Sigh. She didn't believe herself. How could she con-
vince anyone else?

She turned her attention to the last-minute plans for
the gala. After Chadwick returned to the office, he'd
meet with his brother Matthew, who was technically in
charge of planning the event. But a gala for five hundred
of the richest people in Denver? It was all hands on deck.

The checklist was huge, and it required her full attention. She called suppliers, tracked shipments and checked
the guest list.

She ate lunch at her desk as she followed up on her
contacts in the local media. The press was a huge part of
why charities competed for the Beaumont sponsorship.
Few of these organizations had an advertising budget.
Beaumont Brewery put their name front and center for
a year, getting television coverage, interviews and even
fashion bloggers.

She had finished her yogurt and wiped down her desk
by the time Chadwick came back. He looked *terrible*—
head down, hands jammed into his pockets, shoulders
slumped. Oh, no. She didn't even have to ask to know
that the meeting had not gone according to plan.

He paused in front of her desk. The effort to raise his
head and meet her eyes seemed to take a lot out of him.

Serena gasped in surprise at how *lost* he looked. His eyes were rimmed in red, like he hadn't slept in days.

She wanted to go to him—put her arms around him and tell him it'd all work out. That's what her mom had always done when things didn't pan out, when Dad lost his job or they had to move again because they couldn't make the rent.

The only problem was, she'd never believed it when she was a kid. And now, as an adult with a failed long-term relationship under her belt and a baby on the way?

No, she wouldn't believe it either.

God, the raw pain in his eyes was like a slap in the face. She didn't know what to do, what to say. Maybe she should just do nothing. To try and comfort him might be to cross the line they'd crossed on Monday.

Chadwick gave a little nod with his head, as if he were agreeing they shouldn't cross that line again. Then he dropped his head, muttered, "Hold my calls," and trudged into his office.

Defeated. That's what he was. *Beaten.* Seeing him like that was unnerving—and that was being generous. Chadwick Beaumont did not lose in the business world. He didn't always get every single thing he wanted, but he never walked away from a negotiation, a press conference—anything—looking like he'd lost the battle *and* the war.

She sat at her desk for a moment, too stunned to do much of anything. What had happened? What on earth would leave him that crushed?

Maybe it was the hormones. Maybe it was employee loyalty. Maybe it was something else. Whatever it was, she found herself on her feet and walking into his office without even knocking.

Chadwick was sitting at his desk. He had his head

in his hands as if they were the only things supporting his entire weight. He'd shed his suit coat, and he looked smaller for having done it.

When she shut the door behind her, he started talking but he didn't lift his head. "She won't sign off on it. She wants more money. Everything is finalized except how much alimony she gets."

"How much does she want?" Serena had no business asking, but she did anyway.

"Two hundred and fifty." The way he said it was like Serena was pulling an arrow out of his back.

She blinked at him. "Two hundred and fifty dollars?" She knew that wasn't the right answer. Chadwick could afford that. But the only other option was...

"Thousand. Two hundred and fifty thousand dollars."

"A year?"

"A month. She wants three million a year. For the rest of her life. Or she won't sign."

"But that's—that's insane! No one needs that much to live!" The words burst out of her a bit louder than she meant them to, but seriously? Three million dollars a year forever? Serena wouldn't earn that much in her entire lifetime!

Chadwick looked up, a mean smile on his face. "It's not about the money. She just wants to ruin me. If I could pay that much until the end of time, she'd double her request. Triple it, if she thought it would hurt me."

"But why?"

"I don't know. I never cheated on her, never did anything to hurt her. I tried..." His words trailed off as he buried his face in his hands.

"Can't you just buy her out? Make her an up-front offer she can't refuse?" Serena had seen him do that before, with a micro-brew whose beers were undercutting

Beaumont's Percheron Drafts line of beers. Chadwick had let negotiations drag on for almost a week, wearing down the competitors. Then he walked in with a lump sum that no sane person would walk away from, no matter how much they cared about the "integrity" of their beer. Everyone had a price, after all.

"I don't have a hundred million lying around. It's tied up in investments, property…the horses." He said this last bit with an edge, as if the company mascots, the Percherons, were just a thorn in his side.

"But—you have a pre-nup, right?"

"Of *course* I have a pre-nup," he snapped. She flinched, but he immediately sagged in defeat again. "I watched my father get married and divorced four times before he died. There's no way I wouldn't have a pre-nup."

"Then how can she do that?"

"Because." He grabbed at his short hair and pulled. "Because I was stupid and thought I was in love. I thought I had to prove to her that I trusted her. That I wasn't my father. She gets half of what I earned during our marriage. That's about twenty-eight million. She can't touch the family fortune or any of the property—none of that. But…"

Serena felt the blood drain from her face. "Twenty-eight *million*?" That was the kind of money people in her world only got when they won the lottery. "But?"

"My lawyers had put in a clause limiting how much alimony would be paid, for how long. The length of the marriage, fifty thousand a month. And I told them to take it out. Because I wouldn't need it. Like an idiot." That last bit came out so harshly—he really did believe that this was his fault.

She did some quick math. Chadwick had gotten mar-

ried near the end of her first year at Beaumont Brewery—
her internship year. The wedding had been a big thing,
obviously, and the brewery had even come out with a
limited-edition beer to mark the occasion.

That was slightly more than eight years ago. Fifty
thousand—still an absolutely insane number—times
twelve months times eight years was…*only* $4.8 mil-
lion. And somehow, that and another $28 million wasn't
enough. "Isn't there…anything you can do?"

"I offered her one fifty a month for twenty years. She
laughed. *Laughed*." Serena knew the raw desperation
in his voice.

Oh, sure, she'd never been in the position of losing a
fortune, but there'd been plenty of desperate times back
when she was growing up.

Back then, she'd just wanted to know it was going
to be okay. They'd have a safe place to sleep and a big
meal to eat. To know she'd have both of those things the
next day, too.

She never got those assurances. Her mother would
hum "One Day At a Time" over and over when they had
to stuff their meager things into grocery bags and move
again. Then they finally got the little trailer and didn't
have to move any more—but didn't have enough to pay
for both electricity and water.

One day at a time was a damn fine sentiment, but it
didn't put food on the table and clothes on her back.

There had to be a way to appease Chadwick's ex, but
Serena had no idea what it was. Such battles were beyond
her. She might have worked for Chadwick Beaumont for
over seven years, might have spent her days in this office,
might have attended balls and galas, but this was not her
world. She didn't know what to say about someone who
wasn't happy with *just* $32.8 million.

But she could sympathize with staring at a bill that could never be paid—a bill that, no matter how hard your mom worked as a waitress at the diner or how many overtime shifts as a janitor your dad pulled, would never, ever end. Not even when her parents had filed for bankruptcy had it truly ended, because whatever little credit they'd been able to use as a cushion disappeared. She loved her parents—and they loved each other—but the sinking hopelessness that went with never having enough…

That's not how she was going to live. She didn't wish it on anyone, but especially not on Chadwick.

She moved before she was aware of it, her steps muffled by the carpeting. She knew it would be a lie, but all she had to offer were platitudes that tomorrow was a new day.

She didn't hesitate when she got to the desk. In all of the time she'd spent in this office, she'd never once crossed the plane of the desk. She'd sat in front of the massive piece of furniture, but she'd never gone around it.

Today she did. Maybe it was the hormones again, maybe it was the way Chadwick had spoken to her yesterday in that low voice—promising to take care of her.

She saw the tension ripple through his back as she stepped closer. The day before, she'd been upset and he'd touched her. Today, the roles were reversed.

She put her hand on his shoulder. Through the shirt, she felt the warmth of his body. That's all. She didn't even try to turn him as he'd turned her. She just let him know she was there.

He shifted and, pulling his opposite hand away from his face, reached back to grab hers. Yesterday, he'd had all the control. But today? Today she felt they were on equal footing.

She laced their fingers together, but that was as far as

it went. She couldn't make the same kinds of promises he had—she couldn't take care of him when she wasn't even sure how she was going to take care of her baby. But she could let him know she was there, if he needed her.

She chose not to think about exactly what *that* might mean.

"Serena," Chadwick said, his voice raw as his fingers tightened around hers.

She swallowed. But before she could come up with a response, there was a knock on the door and in walked Matthew Beaumont, Vice President of Public Relations for the Beaumont Brewery. He looked a little like Chadwick—commanding build, the Beaumont nose—but where Chadwick and Phillip were lighter, sandier blondes, Matthew had more auburn coloring.

Serena tried to pull her hand free, but Chadwick wouldn't let her go. It was almost as if he wanted Matthew to see them touching. Holding hands.

It was one thing to stick a toe over the business-professional line when it was just her and Chadwick in the office—no witnesses meant it hadn't really happened, right? But Matthew was no idiot.

"Am I interrupting?" Matthew asked, his eyes darting between Serena's face, Chadwick's face, and their interlaced hands.

Of course, Serena would rather take her chances with Matthew than with Phillip Beaumont. Phillip was a professional playboy who flaunted his wealth and went to a lot of parties. As far as Serena could tell, Phillip might be the kind of guy who wouldn't have stopped at a simple touch the day before. Of course, with his gorgeous looks, he probably had plenty of invitations to keep going.

Matthew was radically different from either of his brothers. Serena guessed that was because his mother was Hardwick's second wife, but Matthew was always working hard, as if he were trying to prove he belonged at the brewery. But he did so without the intimidation that Chadwick could wear like a second skin.

With a quick squeeze, Chadwick released her hand and she took a small step back. "No," Chadwick said. "We're done here."

For some inexplicable reason, the words hurt. She didn't know why. She had no good reason for him to defend their touch to his half brother. She had absolutely no reason why she would want Chadwick to defend their relationship—because they didn't have one outside of boss and trusted employee.

She gave a small nod of her head that she wasn't sure either of them saw, and walked out of his office.

Minutes passed. Chadwick knew that Matthew was sitting on the other side of the desk, no doubt waiting for something, but he wasn't up for that just yet.

Helen was out to ruin him. If he knew why, he'd try to make it up to her. But hadn't that pretty much described their marriage? She got her nose bent out of shape, Chadwick had no idea why, but he did his damnedest to make it up to her? He bought her diamonds. She liked diamonds. Then he added rubies to the mix. He'd thought it made things better.

It hadn't. And he was more the fool for thinking it had.

He replayed the conversation with Serena. He hadn't talked much about his divorce to anyone, beyond informing his brothers that it was a problem that would be taking up some measure of his time. He didn't know why he'd told Serena it was his fault that negotiations had gotten to this point.

All he knew was that he'd had to tell someone. The

burden of knowing that this whole thing was a problem he'd created all by himself was more than he could bear.

And she'd touched him. Not like he'd touched her, no, but not like she'd ever touched him before. More than a handshake, that was for damn sure.

When was the last time a woman had touched him aside from the business handshakes that went with the job? Helen had moved out of the master bedroom almost two years before. Not since before then, if he was being honest with himself.

Matthew cleared his throat, which made Chadwick look up. "Yes?"

"If I thought you were anything like our father," Matthew began, his voice walking the fine line between sympathetic and snarky, "I'd assume you were working on wife number two."

Chadwick glared at the man. Matthew was only six months younger than Chadwick's younger brother, Phillip. It had taken several more years before Hardwick's and Eliza's marriage had crumbled, and Hardwick had married Matthew's mother, Jeannie, but once Chadwick's mother knew about Jeannie, the end was just a matter of time.

Matthew was living proof that Hardwick Beaumont had been working on wife number two long before he'd left wife number one.

"I haven't gotten rid of wife number one yet." Even as he said it, though, Chadwick flinched. That was something his father would have said. He detested sounding like his father. He detested *being* like his father.

"Which only goes to illustrate how you are *not* like our father," Matthew replied with an easy-going grin, the same grin that all the Beaumont men had. A lingering gift from their father. "Hardwick wouldn't have cared. Marriage vows meant nothing to him."

Chadwick nodded. Matthew spoke the truth and Chadwick should have taken comfort in that. Funny how he didn't.

"I take it Helen is not going quietly into the night?"

Chadwick hated his half brother right then. True, Phillip—Chadwick's full brother, the only person who knew what it was like to have both Hardwick and Eliza Beaumont as parents—wouldn't have understood either. But Chadwick hated sitting across from the living symbol of his father's betrayal of both his wife and his family.

It was a damn shame that Matthew had such a good head for public relations. Any other half relative would have found himself on the street long ago, and then Chadwick wouldn't have had to face his father's failings as a man and a husband on a daily basis.

He wouldn't have had to face his own failings on a daily basis.

"Buy her out," Matthew said simply.

"She doesn't want money. She wants to hurt me." There had to be something wrong with him, he decided. Since when did he air his dirty laundry to anyone—including his executive assistant, including his half brother?

He didn't. His personal affairs were just that, personal.

Matthew's face darkened. "Everyone has a price, Chadwick." Then, in an even quieter voice, he added, "Even you."

He knew what that was about. The whole company was on pins and needles about AllBev's buyout offer. "I'm *not* going to sell our company tomorrow."

Matthew met his stare head-on. Matthew didn't flinch. Didn't even blink. "You're not the only one with a price, you know. Everyone on that board has a price, too—and probably a far sight less than yours." Matthew paused, looking down at his tablet. "Anyone else would have already made the deal. Why you've stuck by the family name for this long has always escaped me."

"Because, unlike *some* people, it's the only name I've ever had."

Everything about Matthew's face shut down, which made Chadwick feel like an even bigger ass. He remembered his parents' divorce, remembered Hardwick marrying Jeannie Billings—remembered the day Matthew, practically the same age as Phillip, had come to live with them. He'd been Matthew Billings until he was five. Then, suddenly, he was Matthew Beaumont.

Chadwick had tortured him mercilessly. It was Matthew's fault that Eliza and Hardwick had fallen apart. It was Matthew's fault that Chadwick's mom had left. Matthew's fault that Hardwick had kept custody of both Chadwick and Phillip. And it was most certainly Matthew's fault that Hardwick suddenly hadn't had any time for Chadwick—except to yell at him for not getting things right.

But that was a child's cop-out and he knew it. Matthew had been just a kid. As had Phillip. As had Chadwick. Hardwick—it had been all *his* fault that Eliza had hated him, had grown to hate her children.

"I'm...that was uncalled for." Nearly a lifetime of blaming Matthew had made it damn hard to apologize to the man. So he changed the subject. "Everything ready for the gala?"

Matthew gave him a look Chadwick couldn't quite make out. It was almost as if Matthew was going to challenge him to an old-fashioned duel over honor, right here in the office.

But the moment passed. "We're ready. As usual, Ms.

Chase has proven to be worth far more than her weight in gold."

As Matthew talked, that phrase echoed in Chadwick's head.

Everyone did have a price, he realized.

Even Helen Beaumont. Even Serena Chase.

He just didn't know what that price was.

Three

"The Beaumont Brewery has been run by a Beaumont for one hundred and thirty-three years," Chadwick thundered, smacking the tabletop with his hand to emphasize his point.

Serena jumped at the sudden noise. Chadwick didn't normally get this worked up at board meetings. Then again, he'd been more agitated—more abnormal—this entire week. Her hormones might be off, but he wasn't behaving in a typical fashion, either.

"The Beaumont name is worth more than $52 dollars a share," Chadwick went on. "It's worth more than $62 a share. We've got one of the last family-owned, family-operated breweries left in America. We have the pleasure of working for a piece of American history. The Percherons? The beer? That's the result of hard American work."

There was an unsettled pause as Serena took notes. Of

course there was a secretary at the meeting, but Chadwick liked to have a separate version against which he could cross-check the minutes.

She glanced up from her seat off to the side of the hotel ballroom. The Beaumont family owned fifty-one percent of the Beaumont Brewery. They'd kept a firm hand on the business for, well, forever—easily fending off hostile takeovers and not-so-hostile mergers. Chadwick was in charge, though. The rest of the Beaumonts just collected checks like any other stockholders.

She could see that some people were really listening to Chadwick—nodding in agreement, whispering to their neighbors. This meeting wasn't a full shareholders' meeting, so only about twenty people were in the room. Some of them were holdovers from Hardwick's era—handpicked back in the day. They didn't have much power beyond their vote, but they were fiercely loyal to the company.

Those were the people nodding now—the ones who had a personal stake in the company's version of American history.

There were some members—younger, more corporate types that had been brought in to provide balance against the old-boys board of Hardwick's era. Chadwick had selected a few of them, but they weren't the loyal employees that worked with him on a day-to-day basis.

Then there were the others—members brought in by other members. Those, like Harper and his two protégées, had absolutely no interest in Beaumont beer, and they did nothing to hide it.

It was Harper who broke the tense silence. "Odd, Mr. Beaumont. In my version of the American dream, hard work is rewarded with money. The buyout will make you a billionaire. Isn't that the American dream?"

Other heads—the younger ones—nodded in agreement.

Serena could see Chadwick struggling to control his emotions. It hurt to watch. He was normally above this, normally so much more intimidating. But after the week he'd had, she couldn't blame him for looking like he wanted to personally wring Harper's neck. Harper owned almost ten percent of this company, though. Strangling him would be frowned upon.

"The Beaumont Brewery has already provided for my needs," he said, his voice tight. "It's my duty to my company, my *employees*…." At this, he glanced up. His gaze met Serena's, sending a heated charge between them.

Her. He was talking about her.

Chadwick went on, "It's my duty to make sure that the people who *choose* to work for Beaumont Brewery also get to realize the American dream. Some in management will get to cash out their stock options. They'll get a couple of thousand, maybe. Not enough to retire on. But the rest? The men and women who actually make this company work? They won't. AllBev will walk in, fire them all, and reduce our proud history to nothing more than a brand name. No matter how you look at it, Mr. Harper, that's not the American dream. I take care of those who work for me. I reward loyalty. I do not dump it by the side of the road the moment it becomes slightly inconvenient. I cannot be bought off at the expense of those who willingly give me their time and energy. I expect nothing less from this board."

Then, abruptly, he sat. Head up, shoulders back, he didn't look like a man who had just lost. If anything, he looked like a man ready to take all comers. Chadwick had never struck her as a physical force to be reckoned with—but right now? Yeah, he looked like he could fight for his company. To the death.

The room broke out into a cacophony of arguments—
the old guard arguing with the new guard, both arguing with Harper's faction. After about fifteen minutes,
Harper demanded they call a vote.

For a moment, Serena thought Chadwick had won.
Only four people voted to accept AllBev's offer of $52
a share. A clear defeat. Serena breathed a sigh of relief.
At least something this week was going right. Her job
was safe—which meant her future was safe. She could
keep working for Chadwick. Things could continue just
as they were. There was comfort in the familiar, and she
clung to it.

But then Harper called a second vote. "What should
our counteroffer be? I believe Mr. Beaumont said $62 a
share wasn't enough. Shall we put $65 to a vote?"

Chadwick jolted in his seat, looking far more than
murderous. They voted.

Thirteen people voted for the counteroffer of $65 a
share. Chadwick looked as if someone had stabbed him
in the gut. It hurt to see him look so hollow—to know
this was another fight he was losing, on top of the fight
with Helen.

She felt nauseous, and she was pretty sure it had nothing to do with morning sickness. Surely AllBev wouldn't
want to spend that much on the brewery, Serena hoped
as she wrote everything down. Maybe they'd look for a
cheaper, easier target.

Everything Chadwick had spoken of—taking care
of his workers, helping them all, not just the privileged
few, reach for the American dream—that was why she
worked for him. He had given her a chance to earn her
way out of abject poverty. Because of him, she had a
chance to raise her baby in better circumstances than
those in which she'd been raised.

All of that could be taken away from her because Mr. Harper was grinding a forty-year-old ax.

It wasn't fair. She didn't know when she'd started to think that life was fair—it certainly hadn't been during her childhood. But the rules of Beaumont Brewery had been more than fair. Work hard, get promoted, get benefits. Work harder, get a raise, get out of a cube and into an office. Work even harder, get a big bonus. Get to go to galas. Get to dream about retirement plans.

Get to feel secure.

All of that was for sale at $65 a share.

The meeting broke up, everyone going off with their respective cliques. A few of the old-timers came up to Chadwick and appeared to offer their support. Or their condolences. She couldn't tell from her unobtrusive spot off to the side.

Chadwick stood stiffly and, eyes facing forward, stalked out of the room. Serena quickly gathered her things and went after him. He seemed to be in such a fog that she didn't want him to accidentally leave her behind.

She didn't need to worry. Chadwick was standing just outside the ballroom doors, still staring straight ahead.

She needed to get him out of there. If he was going to have another moment like he'd had yesterday—a moment when his self-control slipped, a moment where he would allow himself to be lost—by no means should he have that moment in a hotel lobby.

She touched his arm. "I'll call for the car."

"Yes," he said, in a weirdly blank voice. "Please do." Then his head swung down and his eyes focused on her. Sadness washed over his expression so strongly that it brought tears to her eyes. "I tried, Serena. For you."

What? She'd thought he was trying to save his company—the family business. The family name. What did he mean, he'd tried for *her*?

"I know," she said, afraid to say anything else. "I'll go get the car. Stay here." The driver stayed with the car. The valet just had to go find him.

It took several minutes. During that time, board members trickled out of the ballroom. Some were heading to dinner at the restaurant up the street, no doubt to celebrate their brilliant move to make themselves richer. A few shook Chadwick's hand. No one else seemed to realize what a state of shock he was in. No one but her.

Finally, after what felt like a small eternity, the company car pulled up. It wasn't really a car in the true sense of the word. Oh, it was a Cadillac, but it was the limo version. It was impressive without being ostentatious. Much like Chadwick.

The doorman opened the door for them. Absent-mindedly, Chadwick fished a bill out of his wallet and shoved it at the man. Then they climbed into the car.

When the door shut behind them, a cold silence seemed to grip the car. It wasn't just her security on the line.

How did one comfort a multi-millionaire on the verge of becoming an unwilling billionaire? Once again, she was out of her league. She kept her mouth shut and her eyes focused on the passing Denver cityscape. The journey to the brewery on the south side of the city would take thirty minutes if traffic was smooth.

When she got back to the office, she'd have to open up her resume—that was all. If Chadwick lost the company, she didn't think she could wait around until she got personally fired by the new management. She *needed* uninterrupted health benefits—prenatal care trumped any thought of retirement. Chadwick would understand that, wouldn't he?

When Chadwick spoke, it made her jump. "What do you want?"

"Beg pardon?"

"Out of life." He was staring out his own window. "Is this what you thought you'd be doing with your life? Is this what you wanted?"

"Yes." Mostly. She'd thought that she and Neil would be married by now, maybe with a few cute kids. Being single and pregnant wasn't exactly how she'd dreamed she'd start a family.

But the job? That was exactly what she'd wanted.

So she wasn't breaking through the glass ceiling. She didn't care. She was able to provide for herself. Or had been, anyway. That was the most important thing.

"Really?"

"Working for you has been very...stable. That's not something I had growing up."

"Parents got divorced too, huh?"

She swallowed. "No, actually. Still wildly in love. But love doesn't pay the rent or put food on the table. Love doesn't pay the doctor's bills."

His head snapped away from the window so fast she thought she'd heard his neck pop. "I...I had no idea."

"I don't talk about it." Neil knew, of course. He'd met her when she was still living on ramen noodles and working two part-time jobs to pay for college. Moving in with him had been a blessing—he'd covered the rent for the first year while she'd interned at Beaumont. But once she'd been able to contribute, she had. She'd put all her emphasis on making ends meet, then making a nest egg.

Perhaps too much emphasis. Maybe she'd been so focused on making sure that she was an equal contributor to the relationship—that money would never drive them apart—that she'd forgotten a relationship was more than a bank account. After all, her parents had nothing *but* each other. They were horrid with money, but they loved each other fiercely.

Once, she'd loved Neil like that—passionately. But somewhere along the way that had mellowed into a balanced checkbook. As if love could be measured in dollars and cents.

Chadwick was staring at her as if he'd never seen her before. She didn't like it—even though he no longer seemed focused on the sale of the company, she didn't want to see pity creep into his eyes. She hated pity.

So she redirected. "What about you?"

"Me?" He seemed confused by the question.

"Did you always want to run the brewery?"

Her question worked; it distracted Chadwick from her dirt-poor life. But it failed in that it created another weary wave that washed over his expression. "I was never given a choice."

The way he said it sounded so…cold. Detached, even. "Never?"

"No." He cut the word off, turning his attention back to the window. Ah. Her childhood wasn't the only thing they didn't talk about.

"So, what *would* you want—if you had the choice?" Which he very well might have after the next round of negotiations.

He looked at her then, his eyes blazing with a new, almost feverish, kind of light. She'd only seen him look like that once before—on Monday, when he'd put his finger under her chin. But even then, he hadn't looked quite this…heated. The back of her neck began to sweat under his gaze.

Would he lean forward and put his hand on her again? Would he keep leaning until he was close enough to kiss? Would he do more than just that?

Would she let him?

"I want..." He let the word trail off, the raw need in his voice scratching against her ears like his five-o'clock shadow would scratch against her cheek. "I want to do something for me. Not for the family, not for the company—just for me."

Serena swallowed. The way he said that made it pretty clear what that 'something' might be.

He was her boss, she was his secretary, and he was still married. But none of that seemed to be an issue right now. They were alone in the back of a secure vehicle. The driver couldn't see through the divider. No one would barge in on them. No one would stop them.

I'm pregnant. The words popped onto her tongue and tried frantically to break out of her mouth. That would nip this little infatuation they both seemed to be indulging right in the bud. She was pregnant with another man's baby. She was hormonal and putting on weight in odd locations and wasn't anyone's idea of desirable right now.

But she didn't. He was already feeling the burden of taking care of his employees. How would he react to her pregnancy? Would all those promises to reward her loyalty and take care of her be just another weight he would struggle to carry?

No. She had worked hard to take care of herself. So she was unexpectedly expecting. So her job was possibly standing on its last legs. She would not throw herself at her boss with the hopes that he'd somehow "fix" her life. She knew first-hand that waiting for someone else to fix your problems meant you just had to keep on waiting.

She'd gotten herself into her current situation. She could handle it herself.

That included handling herself around Chadwick.

So she cleared her throat and forced her voice to sound light and non-committal. "Maybe you can find something that doesn't involve beer."

He blinked once, then gave a little nod. He wasn't going to press the issue. He accepted her dodge. It was the right thing to do, after all.

Damn it.

"I like beer," he replied, returning his gaze to the window. "When I was nineteen, I worked alongside the brew masters. They taught me how to *make* beer, not just think of it in terms of units sold. It was fun. Like a chemistry experiment—change one thing, change the whole nature of the brew. To those guys, beer was a living thing—the yeast, the sugars. It was an art *and* a science." His voice drifted a bit, a relaxed smile taking hold of his mouth. "That was a good year. I was sorry to leave those guys behind."

"What do you mean?"

"My father made me spend a year interning in each department, from the age of sixteen on. Outside of my studies, I had to clock in at least twenty hours every week at the brewery."

"That's a lot of work for a teenager." True, she'd had a job when she was sixteen, too, bagging groceries at the local supermarket, but that was a matter of survival. Her family needed her paycheck, plus she got first crack at the merchandise that had been damaged during shipping. She kept the roof over their heads and occasionally put food on the table. The satisfaction she'd gotten from accomplishing those things still lingered.

His smile got less relaxed, more cynical. "I learned

how to run the company. That's what he wanted." She must have given him a look because he added, "Like I said—I wasn't given any choice in the matter."

What his father had wanted—but not what Chadwick had wanted.

The car slowed down and turned. She glanced out the window. They were near the office. She felt like she was running out of time. "If you had a choice, what would you want to do?"

It felt bold and forward to ask him again—to demand he answer her. She didn't make such demands of him. That's not how their business relationship worked.

But something had changed. Their relationship was no longer strictly business. It hadn't crossed a line into pleasure, but the way he'd touched her on Monday? The way she'd touched him yesterday?

Something had changed, all right. Maybe everything.

His gaze bore into her—not the weary look he wore when discussing his schedule, not even the shell-shocked look he'd had yesterday. This was much, much closer to the look he'd had on Monday—the one he'd had on his face when he'd leaned toward her, made the air thin between them. Made her want to feel his lips pressing against hers. Made her want things she had no business wanting.

A corner of his mouth curved up. "What are you wearing on Saturday?"

"What?"

"To the gala. What are you wearing? The black dress?"

Serena blinked at him. Did he seriously *want* to discuss the shortcomings of her wardrobe? "Um, no, actually...." It didn't fit anymore. She'd tried it on on Monday night, more to distract herself from constantly refreshing her email to see if Neil would reply than anything else.

The dress had not zipped. Her body was already changing. How could she not have realized that before she peed on all those sticks? "I'll find something appropriate to wear by Saturday."

They pulled up in front of the office building. The campus of Beaumont Brewery was spread out over fifteen acres, with most of the buildings going back to before the Great Depression.

That sense of permanence had always attracted Serena. Her parents moved so frequently, trying to stay one step ahead of the creditors. The one time Serena had set them up in a nice place with a reasonable rent—and covered the down payment and security deposit, with promises to help every month—her folks had fallen behind. Again. But instead of telling her and giving her a chance to make up the shortfall, they'd done what they always did—picked up in the middle of the night and skipped out. They didn't know how to live any other way.

The Beaumonts had been here for over a century. What would it be like to walk down halls your grandfather had built? To work in buildings your great-grandfather had made? To know that your family not only took care of themselves, but of their children and their children's children?

The driver opened up their door. Serena started to move, but Chadwick motioned for her to sit. "Take the afternoon off. Go to Neiman Marcus. I have a personal shopper there. He'll make sure you're appropriately dressed."

The way he said it bordered on condescending. "I'm sorry—was my black dress inappropriate somehow?"

It had been an amazing find at a consignment shop. Paying seventy dollars for a dress and then another twenty to get it altered had felt like a lot of money, but she'd worn it more than enough to justify the cost, and it had always made her feel glamorous. Plus, a dress like that had probably cost at least five hundred dollars originally. Ninety bucks was a steal. Too bad she wouldn't be able to wear it again for a long time. Maybe if she lost the baby weight, she'd be able to get back into it.

"On the contrary, it would be difficult to find another dress that looks as appropriate on you. That's why you should use Mario. If anyone could find a better dress, it would be him." Chadwick's voice carried through the space between them, almost as if the driver wasn't standing three feet away, just on the other side of the open car door.

Serena swallowed. He didn't have her backed against a door and he certainly wasn't touching her, but otherwise? She felt exactly as she had Monday morning. Except then, she'd been on the verge of sobbing in his office. This? This was different. She wouldn't let her emotions get the better of her today, hormones be damned.

So she smiled her most disarming smile. "I'm afraid that won't be possible. Despite the generous salary you pay me, Neiman's is a bit out of my price range." Which was not a lie. She shopped clearance racks and consignment stores. When she needed some retail therapy, she hit thrift stores. Not an expensive department store. Never Neiman's.

Chadwick leaned forward, thinning the air between them until she didn't care about the driver. "We are attending a work function. Dressing you appropriately is a work-related expense. You will put the dress on my account." She opened her mouth to protest—that was not going to happen—when he cut her off with a wave of his hand. "Not negotiable."

Then, moving with coiled grace, he exited the vehicle. And made the driver shut the door before Serena could follow him out. "Take her to Neiman's," she heard Chadwick say.

No. No, no, no, *no*. This wasn't right. This was wrong on several levels. Chadwick gave her stock options because she did a good job on a project—he did not buy her something as personal, as *intimate*, as a dress. She bought her own clothing with her own money. She didn't rely on any man to take care of her.

She shoved the door open, catching the driver on the hip, and hopped out. Chadwick was already four steps away. "*Sir*," she said, putting as much weight on the word as she could. He froze, one foot on a step. Well, she had his attention now. "I must respectfully decline your offer. I'll get my own dress, thank you."

Coiled grace? Had she thought that about him just moments ago? Because, as Chadwick turned to face her and began to walk back down toward where she was standing, he didn't look quite as graceful. Oh, he moved smoothly, but it was less like an athlete and more like a big cat stalking his prey. *Her.*

And he didn't stop once he was on level ground. He walked right up to her—close enough that he could put his finger under her chin again, close enough to kiss her in broad daylight, in front of the driver.

"You asked, Ms. Chase." His voice came out much closer to a growl than his normal efficient business voice. "Did you not?"

"I didn't ask for a dress."

His smile was a wicked thing she'd never seen on his face before. "You asked me what I wanted. Well, this is what I want. I want to take you out to dinner. I want you to accompany me to this event. And I want you to feel as beautiful as possible when I do it."

She sucked in a breath that felt far warmer than the ambient air temperature outside.

His gaze darted down to her lips, then back up to her eyes. "Because that black dress—you feel beautiful in it, don't you?"

"Yes." She didn't understand what was going on. If he was going to buy her a dress, why was he talking about how she felt? If he was going to buy her a dress and look at her with this kind of raw hunger in his eyes—talk to her in this voice—shouldn't he be talking about how beautiful he *thought* she was? If he was going to seduce her—because that's what this was, a kind of seduction—wasn't he going to tell her she was pretty? That he'd always thought she was pretty?

"It is a work-related event. This is a work-related expense. End of discussion."

"But I couldn't possibly impose—"

Something in him seemed to snap. He did touch her then—not in the cautious way he'd touched her on Monday, and not in the shattered way he'd laced his fingers with hers just yesterday.

He took her by the upper arm, his fingers gripping her tightly. He moved her away from the car door, opened it himself, and put her inside.

Before Serena could even grasp what was happening, Chadwick had climbed in next to her. "Take us to Neiman's," he ordered the driver.

Then he shut the door.

Four

What was wrong with this woman?

That was the question Chadwick asked himself over and over as they rode toward the Cherry Creek Shopping Center, where the Neiman Marcus was located. He'd called ahead and made sure Mario would be there.

Women in his world loved presents. It didn't matter what you bought them, as long as it was expensive. He'd bought Helen clothing and jewelry all the time. She'd always loved it, showing off her newest necklace or dress to her friends with obvious pride.

Of course, that was in the past. In the present, she was suing him for everything he had, so maybe there were limits to the power of gifts.

Still, what woman didn't like a gift? Would flatly refuse to even entertain the notion of a present?

Serena Chase, that's who. Further proving that he didn't know another woman like her.

"This is ridiculous," she muttered.

They were sitting side by side in the backseat of the limo, instead of across from each other as they normally did. True, Serena had scooted over to the other side of the vehicle, but he could still reach over and touch her if he wanted to.

Did he want to?

What a stupid question. Yes, he wanted to. Wasn't that why they were here—he was doing something he wanted, consequences be damned?

"What's ridiculous?" he asked, knowing full well she might haul off and smack him at any moment. After all, he'd forced her into this car with him. He could say this was a work-related expense until he was blue in the face, but that didn't make it actually true.

"This. *You*. It's the middle of the afternoon. On a Wednesday, for God's sake. We have *things* to do. I should know—I keep your schedule."

"I hardly think…" He checked his watch. "I hardly think 4:15 on a Wednesday counts as the middle of the afternoon."

She turned the meanest look onto him that he'd ever seen contort her pretty face. "*You* have a meeting with Sue Colman this afternoon—your weekly HR meeting. *I* have to help Matthew with the gala."

Chadwick got his phone and tapped the screen. "Hello, Sue? Chadwick. We're going to have to reschedule our meeting this afternoon."

Serena gave him a look that was probably supposed to strike fear in his heart, but which only made him want to laugh. Canceling standing meetings on a whim—just because he felt like it?

If he didn't know better, he'd think he was having fun.

"Did the board meeting run long?" Sue asked.

"Yes, exactly." A perfect excuse. Except for the fact that someone might have seen them return to the brewery—and then leave immediately.

"It can wait. I'll see you next week."

"Thanks." He ended the call and tapped on the screen a few more times. "Matthew?"

"Everything okay?"

"Yes, but Serena and I got hung up at the board meeting. Can you do without her for the afternoon?"

There was silence on the other end—a silence that made him shift uncomfortably.

"I suppose I could make do without *Ms. Chase*," Matthew replied, his tone heavy with sarcasm. "Can you?"

If I thought you were anything like our father, Matthew had said the day before, *I'd assume you were working on wife number two.*

Well, he wasn't, okay? Chadwick was not Hardwick. If he were, he'd have Serena flat on her back, her prim suit gone as he feasted on her luscious body in the backseat of this car.

Was he doing that? No. Had he ever done that? *No.* He was a complete gentleman at all times. Hardwick would have made a new dress the reward for a quick screw. Not Chadwick. Just seeing her look glamorous was its own reward.

Or so he kept telling himself.

"I'll talk to you tomorrow." He hung up before Matthew could get in another barb. "There," he said, shoving his phone back into his pocket. "Schedule's clear. We have the rest of the afternoon, all forty-five minutes of it."

She glared at him, but didn't say anything.

It only took another fifteen minutes to make it to the shopping center. Mario was waiting by the curb for them. The car had barely come to a complete stop when he had the back door open. "Mr. Beaumont! What a joy to see you again. I was just telling your brother Phillip that it's been too long since I've had the pleasure of your company."

"Mario," Chadwick said, trying not to roll his eyes at the slight man. Mario had what some might call a *flamboyant* way about him, what with his cutting-edge suit, faux-hawk hair and—yes—eyeliner. But he also had an eagle eye for fashion—something Chadwick didn't have the time or inclination for. Much easier to let Mario put together outfits for him.

And now, for Serena. He turned and held a hand out to her. When she hesitated, he couldn't help himself. He notched an eyebrow in challenge.

That did it. She offered her hand, but she did not wrap her fingers around his.

Fine. Be like that, he thought. "Mario, may I introduce Ms. Serena Chase?"

"Such a delight!" Mario swept into a dramatic bow— but then, he didn't do anything that wasn't dramatic. "An honor to make your acquaintance, Ms. Chase. Please, come inside."

Mario held the doors for them. It was only when they'd passed the threshold that Serena's hand tightened around Chadwick's. He looked at her and was surprised to see something close to horror on her face. "Are you all right?"

"Fine," she answered, too quickly.

"But?"

"I've just…never been in this particular store before. It's…" She stared at the store. "It's different than where I normally shop."

"Ah," he said, mostly because he didn't know what else to say. What if she hadn't been refusing his offer due to stubborn pride? What if there was another reason?

Mario swept around them and clapped his hands in what could only be described as glee. "Please, tell me how I can assist you today." His gaze darted to where Chadwick still had a hold of Serena's hands, but he didn't say anything else. He was far too polite to be snide.

Chadwick turned to Serena. "We have an event on Saturday and Ms. Chase needs a gown."

Mario nodded. "The charity gala at the Art Museum, of course. A statement piece or one of refined elegance? She could easily pull off either with her shape."

Serena's fingers clamped down on Chadwick's, and then she pulled her hand away entirely. Perhaps Mario's extensive knowledge of the social circuit was a surprise to her. Or perhaps it was being referred to in the third person by two men standing right in front of her. Surely it wasn't the compliment.

"Elegant," she said.

"Fitting," Mario agreed. "This way, please."

He led them up the escalator, making small talk about the newest lines and how he had a spotted a suit that would be perfect for Chadwick just the other day. "Not today," Chadwick said. "We just need a gown."

"And accessories, of course," Mario said.

"Of course." When Chadwick agreed, Serena shot him a stunned look. He could almost hear her thinking that he'd said nothing about accessories. He hadn't, but that was part of the deal.

"This way, please." Mario guided them back to a private fitting area, with a dressing room off to the side, a seating area, and a dais surrounded by mirrors. "Champagne?" he offered.

"Yes."

"No." Serena's command was sudden and forceful. At first Chadwick thought she was being obstinate again, but then he saw the high blush that raced across her cheeks. She dropped her gaze and a hand fluttered over her stomach, as if she were nervous.

"Ah." Mario stepped back and cast his critical eye over her again. "My apologies, Ms. Chase. I did not realize you were expecting. I shall bring you a fruit spritzer—non-alcoholic, of course." He turned to Chadwick. "Congratulations, Mr. Beaumont."

Wait—what? *What*?

Chadwick opened his mouth to say something, but nothing came out.

Had Mario just said...*expecting*?

Chadwick looked at Serena, who suddenly seemed to waver, as if she were on the verge of passing out. She did not tell Mario that his critical eye was wrong, that she was absolutely *not* expecting. She mumbled out a pained "Thank you," and then sat heavily on the loveseat.

"My assistant will bring you drinks while I collect a few things for Ms. Chase to model," Mario said. If he caught the sudden change in the atmosphere of the room, he gave no indication of it. Instead, with a bow, he closed the door behind him.

Leaving Chadwick and Serena alone in the silence.

"Did he just say...."

"Yes." Her voice cracked, and then she dragged in a ragged breath.

"And you're..."

"Yes." She bent forward at the waist, as if she could make herself smaller. As if she wanted to disappear from the room.

Or maybe she was on the verge of vomiting and was merely putting her head between her knees.

"And you—you found out this weekend. That's why you were upset on Monday."

"Yes." That seemed to be the only word she was capable of squeezing out.

"And you didn't tell me?" The words burst out of him. She flinched, but he couldn't stop. "Why didn't you *tell* me?"

"Mr. Beaumont, we usually do not discuss our personal lives at the office." At least that was more than a syllable, but the rote way she said it did nothing to calm him down.

"Oh? Were we going to *not* discuss it when you started showing? Were we going to not discuss it when you needed to take maternity leave?" She didn't reply, which only made him madder. Why was he so mad? "Does Neil know?" He was terrified of what she might say. That Neil might not be the father. That she'd taken up with someone else.

He had no idea why that bothered him. Just that it did.

"I…" She took a breath, but it sounded painful. "I sent Neil an email. He hasn't responded yet. But I don't need him. I can provide for my child by myself. I won't be a burden to you or the company. I don't need help."

"Don't lie to me, Serena. Do you have any idea what's going to happen if I lose the brewery?"

Even though she was looking at her black pumps and not at him, he saw her squeeze her eyes shut tight. Of course she knew. He was being an idiot to assume that someone as smart and capable as Serena wouldn't already have a worst-case plan in place. "I'll be out of a job. But I can get another one. Assuming you'll give me a letter of reference."

"Of course I would. You're missing the point. Do you know how hard it'll be for a woman who's eight months pregnant to get a job—even if I sing your praises from the top of the Rocky Mountains?"

She turned an odd color. Had she been breathing, beyond those few breaths she'd taken a moment before?

Jesus, what an ass he was being. *She* was pregnant—so *he* was yelling at her.

Something his father would have done. Dammit.

"Breathe," he said, forcing himself to speak in a quiet tone. He wasn't sure he was nailing "sympathetic," but at least he wasn't yelling. "Breathe, Serena."

She gave her head a tiny shake, as if she'd forgotten how.

Oh, hell. The absolute last thing any of them needed was for his pregnant assistant to black out in the middle of the workweek in an upscale department store. Mario would call an ambulance, the press would get wind of it, and Helen—the woman he was still technically married to—would make him pay.

He crouched down next to Serena and started rubbing her back. "Breathe, Serena. Please. I'm sorry. I'm not mad at you."

She leaned into him then. Not much, but enough to rest her head against his shoulder. Hadn't he wanted this just a few days before? Something that resembled his holding her?

But not like this. Not because he'd lost his temper. Not because she was...

Pregnant.

Chadwick didn't have the first clue how to be a good father. He had a great idea of how to be a really crappy father, but not a good one. Helen had said she didn't want kids, so they didn't have kids. It had been easier that way.

But Serena? She was soft and gentle where Helen, just like his own mother, had been tough and brittle. Serena worked hard and wasn't afraid to learn new things—wasn't afraid to get her hands dirty down in the trenches.

Serena would be a good mother. A *great* mother.

The thought made him smile. Or it would have, if he hadn't been watching her asphyxiate before his very eyes.

"Breathe," he ordered her. Finally, she gasped and exhaled. "Good. Do it again."

They sat like that for several minutes, her breathing and him reminding her to do it again. The assistant knocked on the door and delivered their beverages, but Serena didn't pull away from him and he didn't pull away from her. He sat on his heels and rubbed her back while she breathed and leaned on him.

When they were alone again, he said, "I meant what I said on Monday, Serena. This doesn't change that."

"It changes *everything*." He'd never heard her sound sadder. "I'm sorry. I didn't want anything to change. But it did. *I* did."

They'd lived their lives in a state of stasis for so long—he'd been not-quite-happily married to Helen, and Serena had been living with Neil, not quite happily, either, it turned out. They could have continued on like that forever, maybe.

But everything had changed.

"I won't fail you," he reminded her. Failure had not been an option when he was growing up. Hardwick Beaumont had demanded perfection from an early age. And it was never smart to disappoint Hardwick. Even as a child, Chadwick had known that.

No, he wouldn't fail Serena.

She leaned back—not away from him, not enough to break their contact, but far enough that she could look at him. The color was slowly coming back into her face, which was good. Her hair was mussed up from where her head had been on his shoulder and her eyes were wide. She looked as if she'd just woken up from a long nightmare, like she wanted him to kiss her and make it all better.

His hand moved. It brushed a few strands of hair from her cheek. Then his fingers curved under her cheek, almost as if he couldn't pull away from her skin.

"I won't fail you," he repeated.

"I know you won't," she whispered, her voice shaking.

She reached up—she was going to touch him. Like he was touching her. She was going to put her fingers on his face and then pull him down and he would kiss her. God, how he would kiss her.

"Knock, knock!" Mario called out from the other side of the door. "Is everybody decent in there?"

"Damn."

But Serena smiled—a small, tense smile, but a smile all the same. In that moment, he knew he hadn't let her down yet.

Now he just had to keep it that way.

Five

"Breathe in," Mario instructed as he held up the first gown.

Serena did as she was told. Breathing was the only thing she was capable of doing right now, and even that was iffy.

She'd almost kissed Chadwick. She'd almost let herself lean forward in a moment of weakness and *kiss him*. It was bad enough that she'd been completely unprofessional and had a panic attack, worse that she'd let him comfort her. But to almost kiss him?

She didn't understand why that felt worse than letting him kiss her. But it did. Worse and better all at the same time.

"And breathe *all* the way out. All the way, Ms. Chase. There!" The zipper slid up the rest of the way and she felt him hook the latch. "Marvelous!"

Serena looked down at the black velvet that clung to

every single size-ten curve she had and a few new ones. "How did you know what size I'd need?"

"Darling," Mario replied as he made a slow circle around her, smoothing here and tugging up there, "it's Mario's job to know such things."

"Oh." She remembered to breathe again. "I've never done this before. But I guess you figured that out." He'd guessed everything else. Her dress size, her shoe size—even her bra size. The strapless bra fit a lot better than the one she owned.

"Which part—trying on gowns or being whisked out of the office in the middle of the day?"

Yeah, she wasn't fooling anyone. "Both." Mario set a pair of black heels before her and balanced her as she stepped into them. "I feel like an imposter."

"But that's the beauty of fashion," Mario said, stepping back to look her over yet again. "Every morning you can wake up and decide to be someone new!" Then his face changed. "Even Mario." His voice changed, too— it got deeper, with a thicker Hispanic accent. "I'm really Mario from the barrio, you know? But no one else does. That's the beauty of fashion. It doesn't matter what we were. The only thing that matters is who we are today. And today," he went on, his voice rising up again, "you shall be a queen amongst women!"

She looked at him, more than a little surprised at what he'd said. Was it possible that he really was Mario from the barrio—that he might understand how out of place she felt surrounded by this level of wealth? She decided it didn't matter. All that mattered was that he'd made her feel like she could do this. She felt herself breathe again—and this time it wasn't a strain. "You really are fabulous, you know."

"Oh," he said, batting her comment away with a

pleased grin, "I tell my husband that all the time. One of these days, he's going to believe me!" Then he clapped his hands and turned to the cart that had God only knew how many diamonds and gems on it. "Mr. Beaumont is quite the lucky man!"

But he wasn't. He wasn't the father of her baby and he wasn't even her boyfriend. He was her boss. The walls started to close in on her again.

She needed to distract herself and fast. "Does this happen a lot? Mr. Beaumont showing up with a fashion-challenged woman?" The moment she asked the question, she wished she could take it back. She didn't want to know that she was the latest in a string of afternoon makeovers.

"Heavens, no!" Mario managed to look truly shocked at the suggestion as he turned with a stunning diamond solitaire necklace the size of a pea. "His brother, Mr. Phillip Beaumont? Yes. But not Mr. Chadwick Beaumont. I don't believe he ever even joined his wife on such an afternoon. Certainly not here. I would recall *that*."

Serena breathed again. There wasn't a particularly good reason for that to make her so happy. She had no claim on Chadwick, none at all. And just because he hadn't brought a girl shopping didn't mean he hadn't been seeing anyone else.

But she didn't think he had. He worked too much. She knew. She managed his schedule.

"Now," Mario went on, draping the necklace around her neck and fastening it, "you may have woken up this morning a frugal..." He tilted his head to the side and looked at her suit, now neatly hanging by the door. "Account executive?"

"Close," she said. "Executive assistant."

He snapped his fingers in disappointment, but it didn't

last. "By the time Mario gets done with you, you will *be* royalty."

He held his arm out to her, for which she was grateful—those heels were at least two inches higher than her dress shoes. Then he opened the door and they walked out into the sitting room.

Chadwick was reclined in the loveseat, a glass of champagne in one hand. He'd loosened his tie, a small thing that made him look ten times more relaxed than normal.

Then he saw her. His eyes went wide as he sat up straight, nearly spilling his drink. "Serena...wow."

"And this is just the beginning!" Mario crowed as he led her not to Chadwick but over to the small dais in front of all the mirrors. He helped her up and then guided her in a small turn.

She saw herself in the mirrors. Mario had smoothed her hair out after he'd gotten her suit off her. Her face still looked a little ashen, but otherwise, she couldn't quite believe that was her.

Royalty, indeed. Chadwick had been right. This dress, just like her black dress at home, made her feel beautiful. And after the day she'd had, that was a gift in itself.

She got turned back around and saw the look Chadwick was giving her. His mouth had fallen open and he was now standing, like he wanted to walk right up to her and sweep her into his arms.

"Now," Mario said, although it didn't feel like he was talking to either Serena or Chadwick. "This dress would be perfect for Saturday, but half the crowd will be wearing black and we don't want Ms. Chase to blend, do we?"

"No," Chadwick agreed, looking at her like she hadn't announced half an hour ago that she was pregnant. If anything, he was looking at her like he'd never really seen her before. And he wanted to see a lot more. "No, we don't want that."

"Plus, this dress is not terribly forgiving. I think we want to try on something that has more flow, more grace. More…"

"Elegant," Chadwick said. He seemed to shake back to himself. He backed up to the loveseat and sat again, one leg crossed, appraising her figure again. "Show me what else you've got, Mario."

"With pleasure!"

The next dress was a pale peachy pink number with a huge ball gown skirt and a bow on the back that felt like it was swallowing Serena whole. "A classic style," Mario announced.

"Too much," Chadwick replied, with a shake of his hand. She might have been hurt by this casual dismissal, but then he caught her gaze and gave her a smile. "But still beautiful."

Then came a cornflower blue dress with an Empire waist, tiny pleats that flowed down the length of the gown, and one shoulder strap that was encrusted with jewels. "No necklace," Mario informed her as he handed her dangling earrings that looked like they were encrusted with real sapphires. "You don't want to compete with the dress."

When she came out this time, Chadwick sat up again. "You are…*stunning.*" There was that look again—like he was hungry. Hungry for her.

She blushed. She wasn't used to being stunning. She was used to being professional. Her black dress at home was as stunning as she'd ever gotten. She wasn't sure how she was going to pull off stunning while pregnant. But it didn't seem to be bothering Chadwick.

"This one has a much more forgiving waistline. She'll

be able to wear it for several more months and it'll be easier to get back into it." Mario was talking to Chadwick, but Serena got the feeling that he was really addressing her—greater wearability meant better value.

Although she still wasn't looking at the price tags.

"I don't know where else I'd wear it," she said.

Chadwick didn't say anything, but he gave her a look that made her shiver in the best way possible.

They went through several dresses that no one particularly loved—Mario kept putting her in black and then announcing that black was too boring for her. She tried on a sunflower yellow that did horrible things to her skin tone. It was so bad, Mario wouldn't even let her go out to show Chadwick.

She liked the next, a satin dress that was so richly colored it was hard to tell if it was blue or purple. It had an intricate pattern in lace over the bodice that hid everything she didn't like about her body. That was followed by a dark pink strapless number that reminded her of a bridesmaid gown. Then a blue-and-white off-the-shoulder dress where the colors bled into each other in a way that she thought would be tacky but was actually quite pretty.

"Blue is your color," Mario told her. She could see he was right.

She didn't think it was possible, but she was having fun. Playing dress-up, such as it was. High-end dress-up, but still—this was something she'd had precious little of during her childhood. Chadwick was right—she *did* feel beautiful. She twirled on the dais for him, enjoying the compliments he heaped upon her.

It was almost like…a fairy tale, a rags-to-riches dream come true. How many times had she read some year-old fashion magazine that she'd scavenged from a recycling bin and dreamed about dressing up in the pretty things?

She'd thought she'd gotten that herself with her consignment store dress, but that was nothing compared to being styled by the fabulous Mario.

Time passed in a whirl of chiffons and satins. Soon, it was past seven. They'd spent almost four hours in that dressing room. Chadwick had drunk most of a bottle of champagne. At some point, a fruit-and-cheese tray had been brought in. Mario wouldn't let Serena touch a bite while she was wearing anything, so she wound up standing in the dressing room in her underthings, eating apple slices.

She was tired and hungry. Chadwick's eyes had begun to glaze over, and even Mario's boundless energy was seeming to flag.

"Can we be done?" Serena asked, drooping like a wilted flower in a pale green dress.

"Yes," Chadwick said. "We'll take the blue, the purple, the blue-and-white and…was there another one that you liked, Serena?"

She goggled at him. Had he just listed *three* dresses? "How many times do you expect me to change at this thing?"

"I want you to have all options available."

"One is plenty. The blue one with the single strap."

Mario looked at Chadwick, who repeated, "All three, please. With all necessary accessories. Have them sent to Serena's house."

"Of course, Mr. Beaumont." He gathered up the gowns in question and hurried from the room.

Still wearing the droopy green dress, Serena kicked out of her towering shoes and stalked over to Chadwick. She put her hands on her hips and gave him her very best glare. "*One*. One I shouldn't let you buy me in the first place. I do *not* need three."

He had the nerve to look down at her and smile his ruthless smile, the one that let everyone in the room know that negotiations were finished. Suddenly, she was aware that they were alone and she wasn't wearing her normal suit. "Most women would jump at the chance to have someone buy them nice things, Serena."

"Well," she snapped, unable to resist stamping her foot in protest, "I'm not most women."

"I know." Then—almost as if he were moving in slow motion, he stood and began taking long strides toward her, his gaze fastened on her lips.

She should do...something. Step back. Cross her arms and look away. Flee to the dressing room and lock the door until Mario came back.

Yes, those were all truly things she *should* do.

But she *wanted* him to kiss her.

He slipped one arm around her waist, and his free hand caught her under the chin again. "You're not like any woman I've ever known, Serena. I could tell the very first time I saw you."

"You don't actually remember that, do you?" Her voice had dropped down to a sultry whisper.

His grin deepened. "You were working for Sue Colman in HR. She sent you up to my office with a comparison of new health-care plans." As he spoke, he pulled her in tighter, until she could feel the hard planes of his chest through the thin fabric of the gown. "I asked you what you thought. You told me that Sue recommended the cheaper plan, but the other one was better. It would make the employees happier—would make them want to stay with the brewery. I made you nervous—you blushed—but—"

"You picked the plan I wanted." The plan she'd needed. She'd just been hired full-time. She'd never had health benefits before and she wanted the one with a lower copay and better prescription coverage. She couldn't believe he remembered—but he did.

Her arms went around his chest, her hands flat on his back. She wasn't pushing him away. She couldn't. She wanted this. She had since that day. When she'd knocked on the door, he'd looked up at her with those hazel eyes. Instead of making her feel like she was an interruption, he'd focused on her and asked for her opinion—something he did *not* have to do. She was the lowest woman on the totem pole, barely ranking above unpaid intern— but the future CEO had made her feel like the most important worker in the whole company.

He had looked at her then the same way he was looking at her right now…like she was far more than the most important worker in the company. More like she was the most important woman in the world. "You were honest with me. And what's more than that, you were *right*. It's hard to expect loyalty if you don't give people something to be loyal to."

She'd been devoted to him from that moment on. When he'd been named the new CEO a year later, she'd applied to be his assistant the same day. She hadn't been the most qualified person to apply, but he'd taken a chance on her.

She'd been so thankful then. The job had been a gift that allowed her to take care of herself—to not rely on Neil to pay the rent or buy the groceries. Because of Chadwick, she'd been able to do exactly what she'd set out to do—be financially independent.

She was still thankful now.

Still in slo-mo, he leaned down. His lips brushed against hers—not a fierce kiss of possession, but something that was closer to a request for permission.

Serena took a deep breath in satisfaction. Chadwick's scent surrounded her with the warmth of sandalwood on top of his own clean notes. She couldn't help it—she clutched him more tightly, tracing his lips with her tongue.

Chadwick let out a low growl that seemed to rumble right out of his chest. Then the kiss deepened. She opened her mouth for him and his tongue swept in.

Serena's knees gave in to the heat that suddenly flooded her system, but she didn't go anywhere—Chadwick held her up. Her head began to swim again but instead of the stark panic that had paralyzed her earlier, she felt nothing but sheer desire. She'd wanted that kiss since the very first time she'd seen Chadwick Beaumont. Why on God's green earth had she waited almost eight years to invite it?

Something hard and warm pressed against the front of her gown. A similar weight hung heavy between her legs, driving her body into his. This was what she'd been missing for months. Years. This raw passion hadn't just been gone since Neil had left—it'd been gone for much longer.

Chadwick wanted her. And oh, how she *wanted him*. Wanted to forget about bosses and employees and companies and boards of directors and pregnancies and everything that had gone wrong in her world. This—being in Chadwick's arms, his lips crushed against hers—this was right. So very *right*. Nothing else mattered except for this moment of heat in his arms. It burned everything else away.

She wanted to touch him, find out if the rest of him was as strong as his arms were—but before she could do anything of the sort, he broke the kiss and pulled her into an even tighter hug.

His lips moved against her neck, as if he were smiling

against her. She liked how it felt. "You've always been special, Serena," he whispered against her skin. "So let me show you how special you are. I *want* to buy you all three dresses. That way you can surprise me on Saturday. Are you going to refuse me that chance?"

The heat ebbed between them. She'd forgotten about the dresses—and how much they probably cost. For an insane moment, she'd forgotten everything—who she was. Who he was.

She *absolutely* should refuse the dress, the dinner, the way he had looked at her all afternoon like he couldn't wait to strip each and every dress right off her, and the way he was holding her to his broad chest right now. She had no business being here, doing this—no business letting her attraction to Chadwick Beaumont cloud her thinking. She was pregnant and her job was on the line, and at no point in the past, present or future did she require three gowns that probably cost more than her annual salary.

But then that man leaned backward and cupped her cheek in his palm and said, "I haven't had this much fun in…well, I can't remember when. It was good to get out of the office." His smile took a decade of worry off his face.

She was about to tell him that the champagne had gone to his head—although she was painfully aware that she had no such excuse as to why she'd kissed him back— when he added, "I'm glad I got to spend it with you. Thank you, Serena."

And she had nothing. No refusal, no telling him off, no power to insist that Mario only wrap up one dress and none of the jewelry, no defense that she did not need him to buy her anything because she was perfectly able to buy her own dresses.

He'd had fun. With her.

"The dresses are lovely, Chadwick. Thank you."

He leaned down, his five-o'clock shadow and his lips lightly brushing her cheek. "You're welcome." He pulled back and stuck out his arm just like Mario had done to escort her to the dais. "Let me take you to dinner."

"I…" She looked down at the droopy green dress, which was now creased in a few key areas. "I have to get back to work. I have to go back to being an executive assistant now." Funny how that sounded off all of a sudden. She'd been nothing but an executive assistant for over seven years. Why shouldn't putting the outfit back on feel more…natural?

A day of playing dress-up had gone right to her head. She must have forgotten who she was. She was really Serena Chase, frugal employee. She wasn't the kind of woman who had rich men lavish her with exorbitant gifts. She *wasn't* Chadwick's lover.

Oh God, she'd let him kiss her. She'd kissed him back. What had she *done*?

Chadwick's face grew more distant. He, too, seemed to be realizing that they'd crossed a line they couldn't uncross. It made her feel even more miserable. "Ah, yes. I probably have work to do as well."

"Probably." They might have been playing hooky for a few hours that afternoon, but the world had kept on turning. The fallout from the board meeting no doubt had investors, analysts and journalists burning up the bandwidth, all clamoring for a statement from Chadwick Beaumont.

But more than that, she needed to be away from him. This proximity wasn't helping her cause. She needed to clear her head and stop having fantasies about her boss. Fantasies that now had a very real feel to them—the feeling of his lips against hers, his body pressed to hers.

Fantasies that would probably play out in her dreams that night.

She couldn't accept dinner on top of the dresses. She had to draw the line somewhere.

But she'd already crossed that line.

How much farther would she go?

Six

Chadwick did not sleep well.

He told himself that it had everything to do with the disastrous board meeting and nothing to do with Serena Chase, but what the hell was the point in lying? It had *everything* to do with Serena.

He shouldn't have kissed her. Rationally, he knew that. He'd fired other executives for crossing that very same line—one strike and they were out. For way too long, Beaumont Brewery had been a business where men took all kinds of advantage of the women who worked for them. That was one of the first things he'd changed after his father died. He'd had Serena write a strict sexual harassment policy to prevent exactly this situation.

He'd always taken the higher road. Fairness, loyalty, equality.

He was not Hardwick Beaumont. He would not seduce his secretary. Or his executive assistant, for that matter.

Except that he'd already started. He'd told her he was taking her to the gala. He'd taken her shopping and bought tens of thousands of dollars worth of gowns, jewels and handbags for her.

He'd kissed her. He'd wanted to do so much more than just kiss her, too. He'd wanted to leave that gown in a puddle on the floor and sit back on the loveseat, Serena's body riding his. He wanted to feel the full weight of her breasts in his hands, her body taking his in.

He'd wanted to do something as base and crass as take her in a dressing room, for God's sake. And that was exactly what Hardwick would have done.

So he'd stopped. Thankfully, she'd stopped, too.

She hadn't wanted the dresses. She'd fought him tooth and nail about that.

But the kiss?

She'd kissed him back. Tracing his mouth with her tongue, pressing those amazing breasts against him—holding him just as tightly as he had been holding her.

He found himself in his office by five-thirty the next morning, running a seven-minute mile on his treadmill. He had the international market report up on the screen in front of him, but he wasn't paying a damn bit of attention to it.

Instead, he was wondering what the hell he was going to do about Serena.

She was pregnant. And when she'd come out in those gowns, she'd *glowed*. She'd always been beautiful—a bright, positive smile for any occasion with nary a manipulating demand in sight—but yesterday she'd taken his breath away over and over again.

He was totally, completely, one hundred percent confounded by Serena Chase. The women in Chadwick's world did not refuse expensive clothing and jewelry. They spent their days planning how to get more clothes, better jewels and a skinnier body. They whimpered and pleaded and seduced until they got what they wanted.

That's what his mother had always done. Chadwick doubted whether Eliza and Hardwick had ever really loved each other. She'd wanted his money, and he'd wanted her family prestige. Whenever Eliza had caught Hardwick *in flagrante delicto*—which was often—she'd threaten and cry until Hardwick plunked down a chunk of change on a new diamond. Then, when one diamond wasn't enough, he started buying them in bulk.

Helen had been like that, too. Oh, she didn't threaten, but she did pout until she got what she wanted—cars, clothes, plastic surgery. It had been so much easier to just give in to her demands than deal with the manipulation. In the last year before she filed for divorce, she'd only slept with him when he'd bought her something. Not that he'd enjoyed it much, even then.

Somehow, he'd convinced himself he was fine with that. He didn't need to feel passion because passion left a man wide open for the pain of betrayal. Because there was always another betrayal around the next corner.

But Serena? She didn't cry, didn't whine and didn't pout. She never treated him like he was a pawn to be moved until she got what she wanted, never treated him like he was an obstacle she had to negotiate around.

She didn't even want to let him buy her a dress that made her feel beautiful.

He punched the treadmill up another mile per hour, running until his lungs burned.

He could not be lusting after his assistant and that was final.

This was just the result of Helen moving out of their bedroom over twenty-two months before, that was all.

And they hadn't had sex for a couple of months before that. Yes, that was it. Two years without a woman in his arms—without a woman looking at him with a smile, without a woman who was glad to see him.

Two years was a hell of a long time.

That's all this was. Sexual frustration manifesting itself in the direction of his assistant. He hadn't wanted to break his marriage vows to Helen, even in the middle of their never-ending divorce. Part of that was a wise business decision—if Helen found out that he'd had an affair, even after their separation, she wouldn't sign off on the divorce until he had nothing left but his name.

But part of that was refusing to be like his father.

Except his father totally would have lavished gifts on his secretary and then kissed her.

Hell.

Finally his legs gave out, but instead of the normal clarity a hard run brought him, he just felt more muddled than ever. Despite the punishing exercise, he was no closer to knowing what he was supposed to do when Serena came in for their morning meeting.

Oh, he knew what he wanted to do. He wanted to lay her out on his desk and lavish her curves with all the attention he had. He wanted her to straddle him. He wanted to bring her to a shuddering, screaming climax, and he wanted to hold her afterwards and fall asleep in her arms.

He didn't just want to have sex.

He wanted to have Serena.

Double damn.

He threw himself into his shower without bothering to touch the hot water knob. The cold did little to shock him back to his senses, but at least it knocked his erection down to a somewhat manageable level.

This was beyond lust. He had a need to take care of

her—to *not* fail her. That was why he'd bought her nice things, right? Sure. He was just rewarding her loyalty.

She'd said that her ex hadn't responded to her email. There—that was something he could do. He could get that jerk to step up to the plate and at least acknowledge that he'd left Serena in a difficult situation. Yeah, he liked that idea—making Neil Moore toe the line was a perfectly acceptable way of looking out for his best employee, and it didn't involve kissing her. He doubted that Serena would hold Neil responsible for his legal obligations—but Chadwick had no problem putting that man's feet to the fire.

He shut the water off and grabbed his towel. He was pretty sure he had Neil's information in his phone. But where had he left it?

He rummaged in his pants pocket for a few minutes before he remembered he'd set it down on his desk when he came in.

He opened the door and walked into his office—and found himself face-to-face with Serena.

"Chadwick!" she gasped. "What are you—"

"Serena!" It was then that he remembered the only thing he had on was a towel. He hadn't even managed to dry off.

Her mouth was frozen in a totally kissable "oh," her eyes wide as her gaze traveled down his wet chest.

Desire pumped through him, hard. All he'd have to do would be to drop the towel and show her exactly what she did to him. Hell, at the rate he was going, he wouldn't even have to drop the towel. She wasn't blind and his body wasn't being subtle right now.

"I'm…I'm sorry," she sputtered. "I didn't realize…."

"Just checking my phone." *Just thinking about you.*

He glanced at his clock. She was at least an hour ahead of schedule. "You're early."

"I wanted…I mean, about last night…" She seemed to be trying to get herself back under control, but her gaze kept drifting down. "About the kiss…" A furious blush made her look innocent and naughty at the same time.

He took a step forward, all of his best intentions blown to hell by the look on her face. The same look she'd had the night before when he'd kissed her. She wanted him.

God, that made him feel good.

"What about the kiss?"

Finally, she dropped her gaze from his body to the floor. "It shouldn't have happened. I shouldn't have kissed you. That was unprofessional and I apologize." She rushed through the words in one breath, sounding like she'd spent at least half the night rehearsing that little speech. "It won't happen again."

Wait—what? Was she taking all the blame for that? No. It's not like she'd shoved him against the wall and groped him. He was the one who'd pulled her into his arms. He was the one who'd lifted her chin. "Correct me if I'm wrong, but I thought I was the one who kissed *you.*"

"Yes, well, it was still unprofessional, and it shouldn't have happened while I was on the job."

For a second, Chadwick knew he'd screwed up. She was serious. He'd be lucky if she didn't file suit against him.

But then she lifted her head, her bottom lip tucked under her teeth as she peeked at his bare torso. There was no uncertainty in her eyes—just the same desire that was pumping through his veins.

Then he realized what she'd said—while she was on the job.

Would she be "on the job" on Saturday night? Or off the clock?

"Of course," he agreed. Because, even though she was looking at him like that and he was wearing nothing more than a towel, he was not his father. He could be a reasonable, rational man. Not one solely driven by his baser needs. He could rein in his desires.

Sort of.

"What time shall I pick you up for dinner on Saturday?"

Her lower lip still held captive by her teeth—God, what would it feel like if she bit his lip like that?—he thought he saw her smile. Just a little bit. "The gala starts at nine. We should arrive by nine-twenty. We don't want to be unfashionably late."

He'd take her to the Palace Arms. It would be the perfect accompaniment to the gala—a setting befitting Serena in a gown. "Ms. Chase," he said, trying to use his normal business voice. It was harder to do in a towel than he would have expected. "Please make dinner reservations for two at the Palace Arms for seven. I'll pick you up at six-thirty."

Her eyes went wide again—like they had the day before when he'd informed her he was sending her to Neiman's to get a dress. Like they had when he'd impulsively ordered all three dresses. Why was she so afraid of him spending his money as he saw fit? "But that's…"

"That's what I want," he replied.

And then, because he couldn't help himself, he let the towel slip. Just a little—not enough to flash her—but more than enough to make her notice.

And respond. No, she didn't like it when he flashed his wealth around—but his body? His body appeared to be a different matter entirely. Her mouth dropped open into that "oh" again and then—God help him—her tongue flicked out and traced over her lips. He had to bite down to keep the groan from escaping.

"I'll...I'll go make those reservations, Mr. Beaumont," she said breathlessly.

He couldn't have kept the grin off his face if he tried. "Please do."

Oh, yeah, he was going to take her out to dinner and she was going to wear one of those gowns and he would...

He would enjoy her company, he reminded himself. He did not expect anything other than that. This was not a quid pro quo situation where he bought her things and expected her to fall into bed out of obligation. Sex was not the same as a thank-you note.

Then she held up a small envelope. "A thank-you note. For the dresses."

He almost burst out laughing, but he didn't. He was too busy watching Serena. She took two steps toward the desk and laid the envelope on the top. She was close enough that, if he reached out, he could pull her back into his arms again, right where she'd been the night before.

Except he'd have to let go of the towel.

When had restraint gotten this hard? When had he suddenly had trouble controlling his urges? Hell, when was the last time he'd had an urge he had to control?

Years, really. Long, dry years in a loveless marriage while he ran a company. But Serena woke up something inside of him—and now that it was awake, Chadwick felt it making him wild and impulsive.

The tension in the room was so thick it was practically visible.

"Thank you, Ms. Chase." He was trying to hide behind last names, like he'd done for years, but it wasn't working. All his mouth could taste was her kiss.

"You have Larry coming in for his morning meeting." She didn't step back, but he saw the side-eye she was giving him. "Shall I reschedule him or do you think you can be dressed by then?"

This time, he didn't bother to hold back his chuckle. "I suppose I can be dressed by then. Send him in when he gets here."

She gave a curt nod with her head and, with one more glance at his bare chest, turned to leave.

He couldn't help himself. "Serena?"

She paused at the door, but she didn't look back. "Yes?"

"I…" He snapped off the part about how he wanted her. Even if it was the truth. "I'm looking forward to Saturday."

She glanced back over her shoulder and gave him the same kind of smile she'd had when she'd been twirling in the gowns for him—warm, nervous and excited all at once. "Me, too."

Then she left him alone in his office. Which was absolutely the correct thing to have done.

Saturday sure seemed like a hell of a long time off.

He hoped he could make it.

Serena made sure to knock for the rest of the week.

Not that she didn't want to see Chadwick's bare chest, the light hairs that covered his body glistening with water, his hair damp and tousled….

And certainly not because she'd been fantasizing about Chadwick walking in on her in the shower, leaning her back against the tiled wall, kissing her like he'd kissed her in the store, those kisses going lower and lower until she was blind with pleasure, then her returning the favor….

Right. She knocked extra hard on his door because it was the polite thing to do.

Thursday was busy. The fallout from the board meeting had to be dealt with, and the last-minute plans for the gala could not be ignored. Once Chadwick got his clothes on, she hardly had more than two minutes alone with him before the next meeting, the next phone call.

Friday was the same. They were in the office until almost seven, soothing the jittery nerves of employees worried about their jobs and investors worried about not getting a big enough payout.

She still hadn't heard from Neil. She did manage to get a doctor's appointment scheduled, but it wasn't for another two weeks. If she hadn't heard anything after that, she'd have to call him. That was all.

But she didn't want to think about that. Instead, she thought about Saturday night.

She was not going to fall into bed with Chadwick. Above and beyond the fact that he was still her boss for the foreseeable future, there were too many problems. She *was* pregnant, for starters. She was still getting over the end of a nine-year relationship with Neil—and Chadwick wasn't divorced quite yet. She didn't want whatever was going on with her and Chadwick to smack of a rebound for either of them.

That settled it. If, perhaps in the near future—a future in which Serena was not pregnant, Chadwick was successfully divorced and Serena no longer worked for him because the company had been sold—*then* she could be brazen and call him up to invite him over. *Then* she could seduce him. Maybe in the shower. Definitely near a bed.

But not until then. Really.

So this was just a business-related event. Sure, an extra fancy one, but nothing else had changed.

Except for that kiss. That towel.
Those fantasies.
She was in *so* much trouble.

Seven

Her hair fixed into a sleek twist, Serena stood in her bedroom in her bathrobe and stared at the gowns like they were menacing her. All three were hung on her closet door.

With the price tags still on them.

Somehow, she'd managed to avoid looking at the tags in the store. The fabulous Mario had probably been working overtime to keep them hidden from her.

She had tens of thousands of dollars worth of gowns. Hanging in her house. Not counting the "necessary accessories."

The one she wanted to wear—the one-shoulder, cornflower blue dress that paired well with the long, dangly earrings? That one, on sale, cost as much as a used car. *On sale*! And the earrings? Sapphires. Of course.

I can't do this, she decided. This was not her world and she did *not* belong. Why Chadwick insisted on dressing her up and parading her around was beyond her.

She'd return the dresses and go back to being frugal Serena Chase, loyal assistant. That was the only rational thing to do.

Then her phone buzzed. For a horrifying second, she was afraid it was Neil, afraid that he'd come to his senses and wanted to talk. Wanted to see her again. Wanted frugal, loyal Serena back.

Just because she was trying not to fall head over heels for Chadwick didn't mean she wanted Neil.

She picked up her phone—it was a text from Chadwick.

On my way. Can't wait to see you.

Her heart began to race. Would he wear a suit like he usually did? Would he look stiff and formal or...would he be relaxed? Would he look at her with that gleam in his eye—the one that made her think of things like towels and showers and hot, forbidden kisses?

She should return these things. *All* of them.

She slipped the blue dress off the hanger, letting the fabric slide between her fingers. On the other hand... what would one night hurt? Hadn't she always dreamed about living it up? Wasn't that why she'd always gone to the galas before? It was a glimpse into a world that she longed to be a part of—a world where no one went hungry or wore cast-off clothing or moved in the middle of the night because they couldn't make rent?

Wasn't Chadwick giving her exactly what she wanted?

Why shouldn't she enjoy it? Just for the night?

Fine, she decided, slipping into the dress. One night. One single night where she wasn't Serena Chase, hardworking employee always running away from poverty. For one glorious evening, she would be Serena Chase, queen amongst women. She would be escorted by a man who wouldn't be able to take his eyes off her—a man who made her feel beautiful.

If she ever saw the fabulous Mario again, she was going to hug that man.

She dressed carefully. She felt like she was going too slowly, but she wasn't about to rush and accidentally pop a seam on such an expensive dress. She decided to go with a bolder eye, so she spent more time putting on eyeliner and mascara than she had in the last month.

She'd barely gotten her understated lipstick into the tiny purse that Mario had put with this dress—even though it was a golden yellow—when she heard the knock on the door. "One moment!" she yelled, as she grabbed the yellow heels that had arrived with everything else.

Then she took a moment to breathe. She looked good. She felt good. She was going to enjoy tonight or else. Tomorrow she could go back to being pregnant and frugal and all those other things.

Not tonight. Tonight was hers. Hers and Chadwick's.

She opened the door and felt her jaw drop.

He'd chosen a tux. And a dozen red roses.

"Oh," she managed to get out. The tux was exquisitely cut—probably custom-made.

He looked over the top of the roses. "I was hoping you'd pick that one. I brought these for you." He held the flowers out to her and she saw he had a matching rose boutonnière in his lapel.

She took the roses as he leaned forward. "You look amazing," he whispered in her ear.

Then he kissed her cheek. One hand slid behind her back, gripping her just above her hip. "Simply amazing," he repeated, and she felt the heat from his body warm hers from the inside out.

They didn't have to go anywhere. She could pull him

inside and they could spend the night wrapped around each other. It would be perfectly fine because they weren't at work. As long as they weren't in the office, they could do whatever they wanted.

And he was what she wanted to do.

No. No! She could not let him seduce her. She could not let herself *be* seduced. At least, not that easily. This was a business-related event. They were still on the clock.

Then he kissed her again, just below the dangly earring, and she knew she was in trouble. She had to do something. Anything.

"I'm pregnant," she blurted out. Immediately her face flushed hot. And not the good kind of hot, either. But that was exactly what she'd needed to do to slam on the brakes. Pregnant women were simply not amazing. Her body was crazy and her hormones were crazier and that had to be the *only* reason she was lusting after her boss this much.

Thank heavens, Chadwick pulled back. But he didn't pull away, damn him. He leaned his forehead against hers and said, "In all these years, Serena, I've never seen you more radiant. You've always been so pretty, but now... pregnant or not, you are the most beautiful woman in the world."

She wanted to tell him he was full of it—not only was she not the most beautiful woman in the world, but she didn't crack the top one hundred in Denver. She was plain and curvy and wore suits. Nothing beautiful about that.

But he slipped his hand over her hip and down her belly, his hand rubbing small circles just above the top of her panties. "This," he said, his voice low and serious and intent as his fingers spread out to cover her stomach, "just makes you better. I can't control myself around you anymore and I don't think I want to." As he said it, his hand circled lower. The tips of his fingers crossed over the demarcated line of her panties and dipped down.

The warmth from his touch focused heat in her belly—and lower. A weight—heavy and demanding and pulsing—pounded between her thighs. She didn't want him to stop. She wanted him to keep going until he was pressing against the part of her that was heaviest. To feel his touch explore her body. To make her *his*.

If she didn't know him, she'd say he was feeding her a line of bull a mile long. But Chadwick didn't BS people. He didn't tell them what they wanted to hear. He told them the truth.

He told *her* the truth.

Which only left one question.

Now that she knew the truth, what would she do with it?

The absolute last place Chadwick wanted to be was at this restaurant. The only possible exception to that statement was the gala later. He didn't want to be at either one. He wanted to go back to Serena's place—hell, this restaurant was in a hotel, he could have a room in less than twenty minutes—and get her out of that dress. He wanted to lay her down and show her *exactly* how little he could control himself around her.

Instead, he was sitting across from Serena in one of the best restaurants in all of Denver. Since they'd left her apartment, Serena had been…quiet. He'd expected her to push back against dinner like she'd pushed back against the gown that looked so good on her, but she hadn't. Which was not a bad thing—she'd been gracious and perfectly well-mannered, as he knew she would be—but he didn't know what to talk about. Discussing work was both boring and stressful. Even though this was supposed to be a business dinner, he didn't want to talk about losing the company.

Given how she'd reacted to him touching her stomach—soft and gently rounded beneath the flowing dress—he didn't think making small talk about her pregnancy was exactly the way to go, either. That wasn't making her feel beautiful. At least, he didn't think so. He was pretty sure if they talked about her pregnancy, they'd wind up talking about Neil, and he didn't want to think about that jerk. Not tonight.

Chadwick's divorce was out, too. Chadwick knew talking about exes and soon-to-be-exes at dinner simply wasn't done.

And there was the part where he'd basically professed how he felt about her. Kind of hard to do the chitchat thing after that. Because doing the chitchat thing seemed like it would minimize what he'd said.

He didn't want to do that.

But he didn't know what else to talk about. For one of the few times in his life, he wished his brother Phillip was there. Well, he *didn't*—Phillip would hit on Serena mercilessly, not because he had feelings for her but because she was female. He didn't want Phillip anywhere near Serena.

Still, Phillip was good at filling the silence. He had an endless supply of interesting stories about interesting celebrities he'd met at parties and clubs. If anyone could find *something* to talk about, it'd be his brother.

But that wasn't Chadwick's life. He didn't jet around making headlines. He worked. He went to the office, ran, showered, worked, worked some more and then went home. Even on the weekends, he usually logged in. Running a corporation took most of his time—he probably worked a hundred hours a week.

But that's what it took to run a major corporation. For so long, he'd done what was expected of him—what his father had expected of him. The only thing that mattered was the company.

Chadwick looked at Serena. She was sitting across from him, her hands in her lap, her eyes wide as she looked around the room. This level of luxury was normal for him—but it was fun seeing things through her eyes.

It was fun *being* with her. She made him want to think about something other than work—and given the situation, he was grateful for that alone. But what he felt went way beyond simple gratitude.

For the first time in his adult life—maybe longer— he was looking at someone who meant more to him than the brewery did.

That realization scared the hell out of him. Because, really—who *was* he if he wasn't Chadwick Beaumont, the fourth-generation Beaumont to run the brewery? That was who he'd been raised to be. Just like his father had wanted, Chadwick had always put the brewery first.

But now…things were changing. He didn't know how much longer he'd have the brewery. Even if they fended off this takeover, there might be another. The company's position had been weakened.

Funny, though—he felt stronger after this week with Serena.

Still, he had to say *something*. He hadn't asked her to dinner just to stare at her. "Are you doing all right?"

"Fine," she answered, breathlessly. She did look fine. Her eyes were bright and she had a small, slightly stunned smile on her face. "This place is just so…fancy! I'm afraid I'm going to use the wrong fork."

He felt himself relax a bit. Even though she looked like a million dollars, she was still the same Serena.

His.

No. He pushed that thought away as soon as it cropped up. She was not his—she was only his assistant. That was the extent of his claim to her. "Your parents never dressed you up and took you out to eat at a place like this just for fun?"

"Ah, no." A furious blush raced up her cheeks.

"Really? Not even for a special event?"

That happened a lot. He'd be eating some place nice—some place like this—and a family with kids who had no business being in a five-star restaurant would come in, the boys yanking on the necks of their ties and tipping over the drinks, the girls being extra fussy over the food. He'd sort of assumed that all middle-class people did something like that once or twice.

She looked up at him, defiance flashing in her eyes. The same defiance that had her refusing dresses. He liked it on her—liked that she didn't always bow and scrape to him just because he was Chadwick Beaumont.

"Did your parents ever put you in rags and take you to a food pantry just for fun?"

"What?"

"Because that's where we went 'out to eat.' The food pantry." As quickly as it had come, the defiance faded, leaving her looking embarrassed. She studied her silverware setting. "Sorry. I don't usually tell people that. Forget I said anything."

He stared at her, his mouth open. Had she really just said…*the food pantry?* She'd mentioned that her family had gone through a few financial troubles but—

"You picked the food bank for this year's charity."

"Yes." She continued to inspect the flatware, everything about her closed off.

This wasn't the smooth, flowing conversation he'd wanted. But this felt more important. "Tell me about it."

"Not much to tell." Her chin got even lower. "Poverty is not a bowl full of cherries."

"What happened to your parents?" Not that his parents had particularly loved him—or even liked him—but he'd never wanted for anything. He couldn't imagine how parents could let that happen to their child.

"Nothing. It's just that…Joe and Shelia Chase did everything to a fault. They still do. They're loyal to a fault, forgiving to a fault—generous to a fault. If you need twenty bucks, they'll give you the last twenty they have in the bank and then not have enough to buy dinner or get the bus home. My dad's a janitor."

At this, a flush of embarrassment crept over her. But it didn't stop her. "He'll give you the shirt off his back—not that you'd want it, but he would. He's the guy who always stops when he sees someone on the side of the road with a flat tire, and helps the person change it. But he gets taken by every stupid swindle, every scam. Mom's not much better. She's been a waitress for decades. Never tried to get a better job because she was so loyal to the diner owners. They hired her when she was fifteen. Whenever Dad got fired, we lived on her tips. Which turns out to not be enough for a family of three."

There was so much hurt in her voice that suddenly he was furious with her parents, no matter how kind or loyal they were. "They had jobs—but you still had to go to the food pantry?"

"Don't get me wrong. They love me. They love each other…but they acted as if money were this unknown force that they had no power over, like the rain. Sometimes, it would rain. And sometimes—most of the time—it wouldn't. Money flows into and out of our lives independent of anything we do. That's what they thought. Still think."

He'd never questioned having money, just because there had always been so much of it. Who had to worry about their next meal? Not the Beaumonts, that was for damn sure. But he still worked hard for his fortune.

Serena went on, "They had love, Mom always said. So who needed cars that ran or health insurance or a place to live not crawling with bugs? Not them." Then she looked up at him, her dark brown eyes blazing. "But I do. I want more than that."

He sat there, fully aware his mouth had dropped open in shock, but completely unable to get it shut. Finally, he got out, "I had no idea."

She held his gaze. He could see her wavering. "No one does. I don't talk about it. I wanted you to look at me for what I am, not what I was. I don't want *anyone* to look at me and see a welfare case."

He couldn't blame her for that. If she'd walked into the job interview acting as if he owed her the position because she'd been on food stamps, he wouldn't have hired her. But she hadn't. She'd never played the sympathy card, not once.

"Did Neil know?" Not that he wanted to bring Neil into this.

"Yes. I moved in with him partly because he offered to cover the rent until I could pay my share. I don't think… I don't think he ever really forgot what I'd been. But he was stable. So I stayed." Suddenly, she seemed tired. "I appreciate the dresses and the dinner, Chadwick—I really do. But there were years where my folks didn't clear half of what you paid. To just *buy* dresses for that much…"

Like a bolt out of the blue, he understood Serena in a way he wasn't sure he'd ever understood another person. She was kind and she was loyal—not to a fault, not at the sacrifice of her own well-being—but those were traits that he'd always admired in her. "Why did you pick the brewery?"

She didn't look away from him this time. Instead, she leaned forward, a new zeal in her eyes. "I had internship offers at a couple of other places, but I looked at the employee turnover, the benefits—how happy the workers were. I couldn't bear the thought of changing jobs every other year. What if I never got another one? What if I couldn't take care of myself? The brewery had all these workers that had been there for thirty, forty years—entire careers. It's been in your family for so long...it just seemed like a stable place. That's all I wanted."

And now that was in danger. He wasn't happy about possibly failing to keep the company in family hands, but he had a personal fortune to fall back on. He'd been worried about the workers, of course—but Serena brought it home for him in a new way.

Then she looked up at him through her dark lashes. "At least, that's all I *thought* I wanted."

Desire hit him low and hard, a precision sledgehammer that drove a spike of need up into his gut. Because, unlike Helen and unlike his mother, he knew that Serena wasn't talking about the gowns or the jewels or the fancy dinner.

She was talking about *him*.

He couldn't picture the glamorous, refined woman sitting across from him wearing rags and standing in line at a food pantry. And he didn't have to. That was one of the great things about being wealthy. "I promised you I wouldn't fail you, Serena. I keep my promises." Even if he lost the company—if he failed his father—

he wouldn't leave Serena in a position in which welfare was her only choice.

She leaned back, dropping her gaze again. Like she'd just realized she'd gone too far and was trying to back-track. "I know. But I'm not your responsibility. I'm just an employee."

"The hell you are." The words were out a little faster than he wanted them to be, but what was the point of pretending anymore? He hadn't lied earlier. Something about her had moved him beyond his normal restraint. She was so much *more* than an employee.

Her cheeks took on that pale pink blush that only made her more beautiful. Her mouth opened and she looked like she was about to argue with him when the waiter came up. When the man left with their orders—filet mignon for him, lobster for her—Chadwick looked at her. "Tell me about you."

She eyed him with open suspicion.

He held up his hands in surrender. "I swear it won't have any bearing on how I treat you. I'll still want to buy you pretty things and take you to dinner and have you on my arm at a gala." *Because that's where you belong,* his mind finished for him.

On his arm, in his bed—in his life.

She didn't answer at first, so he leaned forward and dropped his voice. "Do you trust me when I say I'll never use it against you?"

She tucked her lower lip up under her teeth. It shouldn't look so sexy, but on her it did. Everything did.

"Prove it."

Oh, yeah, she was challenging him. But it didn't feel like a battle of wills.

He didn't hesitate. "My dad beat me. Once, with a belt." He kept his voice low, so no one could hear, but it didn't matter. The words ripped themselves out of a place deep inside of his chest.

Her eyes went wide with shock and she covered her open mouth with her hand. It hurt to look at her, so he closed his eyes.

But that was a mistake. He could see his father standing over him, that nice Italian leather belt in his hand, buckle out—screaming about how Chadwick had gotten a C on a math test. He heard the belt whistle through the air, felt the buckle cut into his back. Felt the blood start to run down his side as the belt swung again—all because Chadwick had messed up how to subtract fractions. Future CEOs knew how to do math, Hardwick had reminded him again and again.

That's all Chadwick had ever been—future CEO of Beaumont Brewery. He'd been eleven. It was the only time Hardwick Beaumont had ever left a mark on him, but it was a hell of a mark. He still had the scar.

It was all such a long time ago. Like it had been part of a different life. He thought he'd buried that memory with his father, but it was still there, and it still had the capacity to cause him pain. He'd spent his entire life trying to do what his father wanted, trying to avoid another beating, but what had that gotten him? A failed marriage and a company that was about to be sold out from under him.

Hardwick couldn't hurt him now.

He opened his eyes and looked at Serena. Her face was pale and there was a certain measure of horror in her eyes, but she wasn't looking at him like he feared she would—like she'd forgotten about the man he was now and only saw a bleeding little boy.

Just like he saw a woman he trusted completely, and not a little girl who ate at food pantries.

He kept going. "When I didn't measure up to expectations. As far as I know, he never hit any of his other kids. Just me. He broke my toys, sent my friends away and locked me in my room, all because I had to be the perfect Beaumont to run his company."

"How…how could he do that?"

"I was never his son. Just his employee." The words tasted bitter, but they were the unvarnished truth. "And, like you said, I don't tell people about it. Not even Helen. Because I don't want people to look at me with pity."

But he'd told her. Because he knew she wouldn't hold it against him. Helen would have. Every time they fought, she would have thrown that back in his face because she thought she could use his past to control him.

Serena wouldn't manipulate him like that. And he wouldn't do that to her.

"So," he said, leaning back in his chair, "tell me about it."

She nodded. Her face was still pale, but she understood what he was saying. She understood him. "Which part?"

"All of it."

So she did.

Eight

Serena clung to Chadwick's arm as they swept up the red-carpeted stairs, past the paparazzi and into the Denver Art Museum. Part of her clinginess was because of the heels. Chadwick took huge, masterful strides that she was struggling to keep up with.

But another part of it was how unsettled she was feeling. She'd told him about her childhood. About the one time she and her mom had lived in a women-only shelter for three days because her dad didn't want them to have to sleep on the streets in the winter—but her mom had missed him so much that she'd bundled Serena up and they'd gone looking for him. She'd told him about Missy Gurgin in fourth grade making fun of Serena for wearing her old clothes, about the midnight moves to stay ahead of the due rent, about eating dinner that her mom had scavenged from leftovers at the diner.

Things she'd never told anyone. Not even Neil knew about all of that.

In turn, he'd told her about the way his father had controlled his entire life, about punishments that went way beyond cruel. He'd talked in a dispassionate tone, like they were discussing the weather and not the abuse of a child too young to defend himself, but she could hear the pain beneath the surface. He could act like it was all water under the bridge, but she knew better. All the money in the world hadn't protected Chadwick.

She put her hand over her stomach. No one would ever treat her child like that. And she would do everything in her power to keep her baby from ever being cold and hungry—or wondering where her next meal was coming from.

They walked into the Art Museum. Serena tried to find the calm in her mind. God knew she needed it. She pushed aside the horror of what Chadwick had told her, the embarrassment of sharing her story with him.

This was more familiar territory. She'd come to the Art Museum for this gala for the previous seven years. She knew where the galleries were, where the food was. She'd helped arrange that. She knew how to hold her champagne glass—oh, wait. No champagne for her tonight.

Okay, no need to panic. She was still perfectly at ease. She was only wearing a wildly expensive dress, four-inch heels and a fortune in jewels. Not to mention she was pregnant, on a date with her boss and....

Yeah, champagne would be *great* right about now.

Chadwick leaned over and whispered, "Are you breathing?" in her ear.

She did as instructed, the grin on her face making it easier. "Yes."

He squeezed her hand against his arm, which she found exceptionally reassuring. "Good. Keep it that way."

It was almost ten o'clock. Once they'd started sharing stories at dinner, it had been hard to stop. Serena was both mortified that she'd told any of that to Chadwick and, somehow, relieved. She'd buried those secrets deep, but they hadn't been dead. They'd lived on, terrorizing her like a monster under the bed.

At some point during dinner, she'd relaxed. The meal had been fabulous—the food was a little out there, but good. She'd been able to just enjoy being with Chadwick.

Now they were arriving at the gala slightly later than was fashionable. People were noticing as Chadwick swept her into the main hall. She could see heads tilting as people craned their necks for a better view, could hear the whispers starting.

Oh, this was not a good idea.

She'd loved her black dress because it looked good— but it had also blended, something Mario had forbidden. Now that she was here and standing out in the crowd in a bold blue, she wished she'd gone with basic black. People were *staring*.

A woman wearing a fire engine red gown that matched her fire engine red hair separated from the crowd just as Serena and Chadwick hit the middle of the room. She fought the urge to excuse herself and bolt for the ladies room. Queens amongst women did not hide in the bathroom, and that was *that*.

"There you are," the woman said, leaning to kiss Chadwick on the cheek. "I thought maybe you weren't coming, and Matthew and I would have to deal with Phillip all by ourselves."

Serena exhaled in relief. She should have recognized Frances Beaumont, Chadwick's half sister. She was well liked at the Beaumont Brewery, a fact that had a great deal to do with Donut Friday. Once a month, she personally delivered a donut to every single employee. Apparently, she'd been doing it since she was a little girl. As a result, Serena had heard more than a few of the workers refer to her as "our Frannie."

Frances was the kind of woman people described as "droll" without really knowing what that meant. But her razor-sharp wit was balanced with a good nature and an easy laugh.

Unlike everyone else at the brewery, though, Chadwick didn't seem to relax around his half sister. He stood ramrod straight, as if he were hoping to pass inspection. "We were held up. How's Byron?"

Frances waved her hand dismissively as Serena wondered, *Byron?*

"Still licking his wounds in Europe. I believe he's in Spain." Frances sighed, as if this revelation pained her, but she said nothing else.

Chadwick nodded, apparently agreeing to drop the topic of Byron. "Frannie, you remember Serena Chase, my assistant?"

Frances looked her up and down. "Of course I remember Serena, Chadwick." She leaned over and carefully pulled Serena into a light hug. "Fabulous dress. Where did you get it?"

"Neiman's." Breathing in, breathing out.

Frances gave her a warm smile. "Mario, am I right?"

"You have a good eye."

"Of course, darling." She drawled out this last word until it was almost three whole syllables. "It's a job requirement when you're an antiquities dealer."

"Your dress is stunning." Serena couldn't help but wonder how much it cost. Was she looking at several thousand dollars of red velvet and rubies? The one good thing was that, standing next to Frances Beaumont in that dress, no one was noticing Serena Chase.

Chadwick cleared his throat. She glanced up to find him smiling down at her. Well, no one but him would notice her, anyway.

He turned his attention back to his sister. "You said Phillip is already drunk?"

Frances batted away this question with manicured nails that perfectly matched the color of her dress. "Oh, not yet. But I'm sure before the evening is through he'll have charmed the spirits right out of three or four bottles of the good stuff." She leaned forward, dropping her voice to a conspiratorial whisper. "He's just that charming, you know."

Chadwick rolled his eyes. "I know."

Serena giggled, feeling relieved. Frances wasn't treating her like a bastard at a family picnic. Maybe she could do this.

Then Frances got serious, her smile dropping away. "Chadwick, have you thought more about putting up some money for my auction site?"

Chadwick made a huffing noise of disapproval, which caused a shadow to fall over Frances's face. Serena heard herself ask, "What auction site?"

"Oh!" Frances turned the full power of her smile on Serena. "As an antiquities dealer, I work with a lot of people in this room who'd prefer not to pay the full commission to Christie's auction house in New York, but who would never stoop to the level of eBay."

Ouch. Serena had bought more than a few things off the online auction site.

"So," Frances went on, unaware of the impact of her words on Serena, "I'm funding a new venture called Beaumont Antiquities that blends the cachet of a traditional art auction house with the power of social media. I have some partners who are handling the more technical aspects of building our platform, while I'm bringing the family name and my *extensive* connections to the deal." She turned back to Chadwick. "It's going to be a success. This is your chance to get in on the ground floor. And we could use the Chadwick Beaumont Seal of Approval. It'd go a long way to help secure additional funding. Think of it. A Beaumont business that has nothing to do with beer!"

"I like beer," Chadwick said. His tone was probably supposed to be flat, but it actually came out sounding slightly wounded, as if Frances had just told him his life's work was worthless.

"Oh, you know what I mean."

"You always do this, Frannie—investing in the 'next big idea' without doing your homework. An exclusive art auction site? In this market? It's not a good idea. If I were you, I'd get out now before you lose everything. Again."

Frances stiffened. "I haven't lost *everything*, thank you very much."

Chadwick gave her a look that was surprisingly paternal. "And yet, I've had to bail you out how many times?" Frances glared at him. Serena braced for another cutting remark, but then Chadwick said, "I'm sorry. Maybe this one will be a success. I wish you the best of luck."

"Of course you do. You're a good brother." Instantly, her droll humor was back, but Serena could see a shadow of disappointment in her eyes. "We're Beaumonts. You're the only one of us who behaves—well, you and maybe Matthew." She waved her hand in his general direction. "All respectable, while the rest of us are desperately trying to be dissolute wastrels." Her gaze cut between Chadwick and Serena. "Speaking of, there's Phillip now."

Before Serena could turn, she felt a touch slide down her bare arm. Then Phillip Beaumont walked around her, his fingers never leaving her skin. He was quite the golden boy. Only an inch shorter than his brother, he wore a tux without a bow tie. It made him look disheveled and carefree—which, according to all reports, he was. Where Chadwick was more of a sandy-blond, Phillip's coloring was brighter, as if he'd been born for people to look at him.

Phillip took her hand in his and bent low over it. "*Mademoiselle*," he said as he held the back of her hand against his lips.

An uncontrollable shiver raced through her body. She did not particularly like Phillip—he caused Chadwick no end of grief—but Frances was one-hundred-percent right. He was exceedingly charming.

He looked up at Serena, his lips curled into the kind of grin that pronounced him fully aware of the effect he was having on her. "*Where* did you come from, enchantress? And, perhaps more importantly, why are you on *his* arm?"

Enchantress? That was a new one. And also a testament to Mario's superpowers. Phillip stopped by the office on a semi-regular basis to have meetings with Chadwick and Matthew about his position as head of special promotions for the brewery. She'd talked to him face-to-face dozens, if not hundreds, of times.

Chadwick made a sound that was somewhere between clearing his throat and growling. "Phillip, you remember Serena Chase, my executive assistant."

If Phillip was embarrassed that he hadn't recognized her, he gave no sign of it. He didn't even break eye contact with her. Instead, he favored her with the kind of smile that probably made the average woman melt into his bed. As it was, she was feeling a little dazzled by his sheer animal magnetism.

"How could I forget Ms. Chase? You are," he went on, leaning into her, "*unforgettable.*"

Desperate, she looked at Frances, who gave a small shrug.

"That's *enough.*" No mistaking it this time—that was nothing but a growl from Chadwick.

If Chadwick had growled at anyone else like that, he would have sent them diving for cover. But not Phillip. Good heavens, he didn't even look ruffled. He did give her a sly little wink before he touched her hand to his lips again. Chadwick tensed next to her and she wondered if a brawl was about to break out.

But then he released his grip on her hand and turned his full attention to his brother. Serena heaved a sigh of relief. No wonder Phillip had such a reputation as a ladies' man.

"So, news," he said in a tone that was only slightly less sultry than the one he'd been using on her. "I bought a horse!"

"Another one?" Frances and Chadwick said at the same time. Clearly, this was something that happened often.

"You've got to be kidding me." Chadwick looked… murderous. There really was no other way to describe it. He looked like he was going to throttle his brother in the middle of the Art Museum. "I don't suppose this one was only a few thousand?"

"Chad—hear me out." At this use of his shortened name, Chadwick flinched. Serena had never heard anyone call him that but Phillip. "This is an Akhal-Teke horse."

"*Gesundheit,*" Frances murmured.

"A *what*?" Chadwick was now clutching her fingers against his arm in an almost desperate way. "How much?"

"This breed is extremely rare," Phillip went on. "Only about five thousand in the world. From Turkmenistan!"

Serena felt like she was at a tennis match, her head was turning back and forth between the two brothers so quickly. "Isn't that in Asia, next to Afghanistan?"

Phillip shot her another white-hot look and matching smile. "Beautiful *and* smart? Chadwick, you lucky dog."

"I swear to God," Chadwick growled.

"People are staring," Frances added in a light, sing-song tone. Then, looking at Serena for assistance, she laughed as if this were a great joke.

Serena laughed as well. She'd heard Chadwick and Phillip argue before, but that was usually behind Chadwick's closed office door. Never in front of her. Or in front of anyone else, for that matter.

For once, Phillip seemed to register the threat. He took an easy step back and held out his hands in surrender. "Like I was saying—this Akhal-Teke. They're most likely the breed that sired the Arabians. Very rare. Only about five hundred in this country, and most of those come from Russian stock. Kandar's Golden Sun isn't a Russian Akhal-Teke."

"*Gesundheit*," Frances murmured again. She looked at Serena with a touch of desperation, so they both laughed again.

"He's from Turkmenistan. An incredible horse. One to truly found a stable on."

Chadwick pinched the bridge of his nose. "How much?"

"Only seven." Phillip stuck out his chest, as if he were proud of this number.

Chadwick cracked open one eye. "Thousand, or hundred thousand?"

Serena tried not to gape. Seven thousand for a horse wasn't too much, she guessed. But seven *hundred* thousand? That was a lot of money.

Phillip didn't say anything. He took a step back, though, and his smile seemed more...forced.

Chadwick took a step forward. "Seven *what*?"

"You know, one Akhal-Teke went for fifty million—and that was in 1986 dollars. The most expensive horse ever. Kandar's Golden Sun—"

That was as far as he got. Chadwick cut him off with a shout. "You spent seven *million* on a horse while I'm working my ass off to keep the company from being sold to the wolves?"

Everything about the party stopped—the music, the conversations, the movement of waiters carrying trays of champagne.

Someone hurried toward them. It was Matthew Beaumont. "Gentlemen," he hissed under his breath. "We are having a *charity* event here."

Serena put her hand on Chadwick's arm and gave it a gentle tug. "A very good joke, Phillip," she said in a slightly too-loud voice.

Frances caught Serena's eye and nodded in approval. "Chadwick, I'd like to introduce you to the director of the food bank, Miriam Young." She didn't know where, exactly, the director of the food bank was. But she was sure Ms. Young wanted to talk with Chadwick. Or, at least, had wanted to talk to him before he'd started yelling menacingly at his relatives.

"Phillip, did I introduce you to my friend Candy?" Frances added, taking her brother by the arm and pulling him in the opposite direction. "She's *dying* to meet you."

The two brothers held their poses for a moment longer, Chadwick glaring at Phillip, the look on Phillip's face almost daring Chadwick to hit him in full view of the assembled upper crust of Denver society.

Then the men parted. Matthew walked on the other side of Chadwick, ostensibly to lead the way to the director. Serena got the feeling it was more to keep Chadwick from spinning and tackling his brother.

"Serena," Matthew said simply. "Nicely done. *Thus far*," he added in a heavy tone, "the evening has been a success. Now if we can just get through it without a brawl breaking out—"

"I'm fine," Chadwick snapped, sounding anything but. "I'm just *fine*."

"Not fine," Matthew muttered, guiding them into a side gallery. "Why don't I get you a drink? Wait here," he said, parking Chadwick in front of a Remington statue. "Do *not* move." He looked at Serena. "Okay?"

She nodded. "I've got him."

She hoped.

Nine

Chadwick had never really believed the old cliché about being so mad one saw red. Turns out, he'd just never been mad enough, because right now, the world was drenched in red-hot anger.

"How could he?" he heard himself mutter. "How could he just buy a horse for that much money without even thinking about the consequences?"

"Because," a soft, feminine voice said next to him, "he's not you."

The voice calmed him down, and some of the color bled back into the world. He realized Serena was standing next to him. They were in a nearly empty side gallery, in front of one of the Remington sculptures that made the backbreaking work of herding cattle look glorious.

She was right. Hardwick had never expected anything from Phillip. Never even noticed him, unless he did something outrageous.

Like buy a horse no one had ever heard of for seven million damn dollars.

"Remind me again why I work myself to death so that he can blow the family fortune on horses and women? So Frances can sink money into another venture that's bound to fail before it gets off the ground? Is that all I'm good for? A never-ending supply of cash?"

Delicate fingers laced through his, holding him tightly. "Maybe," Serena said, her voice gentle, "you don't have to work yourself to death at all."

He turned to her. She was staring at the statue as if it were the most interesting thing in the world.

Phillip had done whatever the hell he wanted since he was a kid. It hadn't mattered what his grades were, who his friends were, how many sports cars he had wrecked. Hardwick just hadn't cared. He'd been too focused on Chadwick.

"I..." He swallowed. "I don't know how else to run this company." The admission was even harder than what he'd shared over dinner. "This is what I was raised to do."

She tilted her head to one side, really studying the bronze. "Your father died while working, didn't he?"

"Yes." Hardwick had keeled over at a board meeting, dead from the heart attack long before the ambulance had gotten there. Which was better, Chadwick had always figured, than him dying in the arms of a mistress.

She tilted her head in the other direction, not looking at him but still holding his hand. "I rather like you alive."

"Do you?"

"Yes," she answered slowly, like she really had to think about it. But then her thumb moved against the palm of his hand. "I do."

Any remaining anger faded out of his vision as the room—the woman in it—came into sharp focus.

"You told me a few days ago," she went on, her voice quiet in the gallery, "that you wanted to do something for yourself. Not for the family, not for the company. Then you spent God only knows how much on everything I'm wearing." He saw the corner of her mouth curve up into a sly smile. "Except for a few zeros, this isn't so different, is it?"

"I don't need to spend money to be happy like he does."

"Then why am I wearing a fortune's worth of finery?"

"Because." He hadn't done it because it made him happy. He'd done it to see her look like this, to see that genuine smile she always wore when she was dressed to the nines. To know he could still *make* a woman smile.

He'd done it to make her happy. *That* was what made him happy.

She shot him a sidelong glance that didn't convey annoyance so much as knowing—like that was exactly what she'd expected him to say. "You are an impossibly stubborn man when you want to be, Chadwick Beaumont."

"It has been noted."

"What do you want?"

Her.

He'd wanted her for years. But because he was not Hardwick Beaumont, he'd never once pursued her.

Except now he was. He was walking a fine line between acceptable actions and immoral, unethical behavior.

What he really wanted, more than anything, was to step over that line entirely.

She looked up at him through her thick lashes, waiting for an answer. When he didn't give her one, she sighed. "The Beaumonts are an intelligent lot, you know. They'll learn how to survive. You don't have to protect them.

Don't work for them. They won't ever appreciate it because they didn't earn it themselves. Work for you." She reached up and touched his cheek. "Do what makes *you* happy. Do what *you* want."

She did realize what she was telling him, didn't she? She had to—her fingers wrapped around his, her palm pressed against his cheek, her dark brown eyes looking into his with a kind of peace that he couldn't remember ever feeling.

What he wanted was to leave this event behind, drive her home, and make love to her all night long. She *had* to know that was all he wanted—however not-divorced he was, pregnant she was, or employed she was by him.

Was she giving him permission? He would not trap his assistant into any sexual relationship. That wasn't him.

God, he wanted her permission. *Needed* it. Always had.

"Serena—"

"Here we are." Matthew strode into the gallery leading Miriam Young, the director of the Rocky Mountain Food Bank, and a waiter with a tray of champagne glasses. He gave Serena a look that was impossible to miss. "How is everything?"

She withdrew her hand from his cheek. "Fine," she said, with one of those beautiful smiles.

Matthew made the introductions and Serena politely declined the champagne. Chadwick only half paid attention. Her words echoed around his head like a loose bowling ball in the trunk of a car.

Don't work for them. Work for you.

Do what makes you happy.

She was right. It was high time he did what he wanted—above and beyond one afternoon.

It was time to seduce his assistant.

* * *

Standing in four-inch heels for two hours turned out to be more difficult than Serena had anticipated. She resorted to shifting from foot to foot as she and Chadwick made small talk with the likes of old-money billionaires, new-money billionaires, governors, senators and foundation heads. Most of the men were in tuxes like Chadwick's, and most of the women were in gowns. So she blended in well enough.

Chadwick had recovered from the incident with Phillip nicely. She'd like to think that had something to do with their conversation in the gallery. With the way she'd told him to do what he wanted and the way he'd looked at her like the only thing he wanted to do was *her*.

She knew there was a list of reasons not to want him back. But she was tired of those reasons, tired of thinking she couldn't, she *shouldn't*.

So she didn't. She focused on how painful those beautiful, beautiful shoes were. It kept her in the here and now.

Shoes aside, the evening had been delightful. Chadwick had introduced her as his assistant, true, but all the while he'd let one of his hands rest lightly on her lower back. She'd gotten a few odd looks, but no one had said anything. That probably had more to do with Chadwick's reputation than anything else, but she wasn't about to question it. Even without champagne, she'd been able to fall into small talk without too much panic.

She'd had a much nicer time than when she used to come with Neil. Then, she'd stood on the edge of the crowd, judiciously sipping her champagne and watching the crowd instead of interacting with it. Neil had always talked to people—always looking for another sponsor for his golf game—but she'd never felt like she was a part of the party.

Chadwick had made her a part of it this time. She wasn't sure she'd ever truly feel like she fit in with the high roller crowd, but she hadn't felt like an interloper. That counted for a great deal.

The evening was winding down. The crowd was trailing out. She hadn't seen Phillip leave, but he was nowhere to be seen. Frances had bailed almost an hour before. Matthew was the only other Beaumont still there, and he was deep in discussion with the caterers.

Chadwick shook hands with the head of the Centura Hospital System and turned to her. "Your feet hurt."

She didn't want to seem ungrateful for the shoes, but she wasn't sure her toes would ever be the same. "Maybe just a little."

He gave her a smile that packed plenty of heat. But it wasn't indiscriminately flirtatious, like his brother's. All night long, that goodness had been directed at only one woman.

Her.

He slid a hand around her waist and began guiding her toward the door. "I'll drive you home."

She grinned at this statement. "Don't worry. I didn't snag a ride with anyone else."

"Good."

The valet brought up Chadwick's Porsche, but he insisted on holding the door for her. Then he was in the car and they were driving at a higher-than-average speed, zipping down the highway like he had someplace to be.

Or like he couldn't wait to get her home.

The ride was quick, but silent. What was going to happen next? More importantly, what did she want to happen next? And—most importantly of all—what would she *let* happen?

Because she wanted this perfect evening to end perfectly. She wanted to have one night with him, to touch the body she'd only gotten a glimpse of, to feel beautiful and desirable in his arms. She didn't want to think about pregnancies or exes or jobs. It was Saturday night and she was dressed to the nines. On Monday, maybe they could go back to normal. She'd put on her suit and follow the rules and try not to think about the way Chadwick's touch made her feel things she'd convinced herself she didn't need.

Soon enough, he'd pulled up outside her apartment. His Porsche stuck out like a sore thumb in the parking lot full of minivans and late-model sedans. She started to open her door, but he put a hand on her arm. "Let me."

Then he hopped out, opened her door and held his hand out for her. She let him help her out of the deep seats of his car.

Then they stood there.

His strong hand held tight to hers as he pulled her against his body. She looked up into his eyes, feeling lightheaded without a drop of champagne. All night long, he'd only had eyes for her—but they'd been surrounded by people.

Now they were alone in the dark.

He reached up and traced the tips of his fingers over her cheek. Serena's eyelids fluttered shut at his touch.

"I'll walk you to your door," he said, his voice thick with strain. He stroked her skin—a small movement, similar to the way he'd touched her on Monday.

But this was different. Everything was different now.

This was the moment. This was her decision. She didn't want sex with Chadwick to be one of those things that "just happened," like her pregnancy. She was in control of her own life. She made the choices.

She could thank him for the lovely evening and tell

him she'd see him bright and early Monday morning. She could even make a little joke about seeing him in a towel again. Then she could walk into her apartment, close the door and...

Maybe never have another moment—another chance—to be with Chadwick.

She made her choice. She would not regret it.

She opened her eyes. Chadwick's face was inches from hers, but he wasn't pressing her to anything. He was waiting for her.

She wouldn't make him wait any longer. "Would you like to come in?"

He tensed against her. "Only if I can stay."

She kissed him then. She leaned up in the painful, beautiful shoes and pressed her lips to his. There was no "kissing him back," no "waiting for him to make the first move."

This was going to happen because she wanted it to. She'd wanted it for years and she was darn tired of waiting. That was reason enough.

"I'd like that."

The next thing she knew, Chadwick had physically swept her off her feet and was carrying her up to her door. When she gave him a quizzical look, he grinned sheepishly and said, "I know your feet hurt."

"They do."

She draped her arms around his neck and held on as he took the stairs, carrying her as if she were one of the skinny women from the party instead of someone whose size-ten body was getting bigger every day. But then, she'd seen all his muscles a few days before. If anyone could carry her, it was him. His chest was warm and hard against her body.

Things began to tighten. Her nipples tensed underneath the gown, and that heavy weight between her legs seemed to be pulling her down into his body. Oh, yes. She wanted him. But the thing that was different from all her time with Neil was how intense it felt to want Chadwick.

Obviously, it'd only been a few months since the last time she'd had sex with Neil. Just about three months. That was how far along she was. But she hadn't felt the physical weight of desire for much, much longer than that. She couldn't remember the last time just thinking about sex with Neil had turned her on this much. Maybe it was her crazy hormones—or maybe Chadwick did this to her. Maybe he'd always done this to her and she'd forced herself to ignore the attraction because falling for her boss just wasn't convenient.

He set her down at the door so she could get her key out of the tiny purse. But he didn't let her go. He put his hands on her hips and pulled her back into his front. They didn't talk, but the huge bulge that pressed against her backside said *lots* of things, loud and clear.

She got the door open and they walked inside. She kicked off the pretty shoes, which made Chadwick loom an extra four inches over her. He hadn't let go of her. His hands were still on her hips. He was *grabbing* her in a way that was quickly going from gentle to possessive. The way he filled his palms with her hips didn't make her feel fat. It made her feel like he couldn't get enough of her—he couldn't help himself.

Yes. That was what she needed—to be wanted so much that he couldn't control himself.

He leaned down, his mouth against her ear. "I've been waiting for you for years." The strain of the wait made his voice shake. He pulled her hips back again, the ridge in his pants unmistakable. "*Years*, Serena."

"Me, too." Her voice came out breathy, barely above a

whisper. She reached behind her back and slid her hand up the bulge. "Is that for me?"

"Yes," he hissed, his breath hot against her skin. One hand released a hip and found her breast instead. Even through the strapless bra, he found her pointed nipple and began to tease it. "You deserve slow and sensual, but I need you too much right now."

As if to prove his point, he set his teeth against her neck and bit her skin. Not too hard, but the feeling of being consumed by desire—by him—crashed through her. Her knees began to shake.

"Slow later," she agreed, wiggling her bottom against him.

With a groan, he stepped away from her. She almost toppled over backward, but then his hands were unzipping her dress. The gown slid off her one shoulder and down to the ground with a soft rustle.

She was extra glad she hadn't gone with the Spanx. Bless Mario's heart for putting her in a dress that didn't require them. Instead, a matching lacy thong had arrived with the bra. Which meant Chadwick currently had one heck of a view. She didn't know if she should strut, or pivot so he couldn't see her bottom.

Once the gown was gone, she stepped free of it. Chadwick moaned. "Serena," he got out as he slid his hands over her bare backside. "You are…amazing." His fingers gripped her skin, and he pressed his mouth to the space between her neck and her shoulder.

Strut, she decided. Nothing ruined good sex like being stupidly self-conscious when he already thought she was amazing. She pulled away from him before he could take away her power to stand.

"This way," she said over her shoulder as she, yes, *strutted* toward the bedroom, her hips swaying.

Chadwick made a noise behind her that she took as a compliment, before following her.

She headed toward the bed, but he caught up with her. He grabbed her hips again. "You are better than I thought," he growled as his hands slipped underneath the lace of the thong. He pulled the panties down, his palms against her legs. "I've dreamed of having you like this."

"Like how?"

He nimbly undid her bra, tossing it aside. She was naked. He was not.

He directed her forward, but not toward the bed. Instead, he pushed her in the direction of her dresser.

The one with the big mirror over it.

Serena gasped at the sight they made. Her, nude. Him, still in his tux, towering over her.

"This. Like this." He bent his head until his lips were on her neck again, just below the dangling earrings. "Is this okay?" he murmured against her skin.

"Yes." She couldn't take her eyes off their reflections, the way her pale skin stood out against his dark tux. The way his arms wrapped around her body, his hands cradled her breasts. The way his mouth looked as he kissed her skin.

The driving weight of desire between her legs pounded with need. "Yes," she said again, reaching one arm over her head and tangling her fingers in his hair. "Just like this."

"Good. So good, Serena." Without the bra, she could feel the pads of his fingertips trace over her sensitive nipple, pulling until it went stiff with pleasure.

She moaned, letting her head fall back against his shoulder. "Just like that," she whispered.

Then his other hand traced lower. This time, he didn't pause to stroke her stomach. His fingers parted her neatly trimmed hair and pressed against her heaviest, hottest place.

"Oh, Chadwick," she gasped as he moved his fingers in small, knowing circles, his other hand stroking her nipple, his mouth finding the sensitive spot under her ear—his bulge rubbing against her.

Her knees gave, but she didn't go far. Her wet center rode heavy on his hand as his other arm caught her under both breasts.

"Put your hands on the dresser," he told her. His voice was shaking as badly as her knees were, which made her smile. He might be pushing her to the brink, but she was pulling him along right behind her. "Don't close your eyes."

"I won't." She leaned forward and braced herself on the dresser. "I want to see what you do to me."

"Yeah," he groaned, a look of pure desire on his face as he met her gaze in the mirror. A finger slipped inside. So much, but not enough. She needed more. "You're so ready for me." Then she felt him lean back and work his own zipper.

"Next time, I get to do that for you."

"Any time you want to strip me down, you just let me know. Hold on, okay?" Then he withdrew his fingers.

She watched as he removed a condom from his jacket pocket. It wasn't like she could get more pregnant than she already was, but she appreciated that he didn't question protecting her.

He rolled the condom on and leaned into her. She quivered as she waited for his touch. He bent forward, placing a kiss between her shoulder blades. Then he was against her. Sliding into her.

Serena sucked in air as he filled her. And filled her. And *filled* her. In the mirror, her eyes locked onto his as he entered her. She almost couldn't take it. "Oh, Chadwick," she panted as her body took him in. "Oh—oh—*oh*!"

The unexpected orgasm shook her so hard that she almost pulled off him—but he held her. "Yeah," he groaned. "You feel so beautiful, Serena. So beautiful."

He gripped her hips as he slid almost all the way out before he thrust in again. "Okay?" he asked.

"Better than okay," she managed to get out, wiggling against him. The boldness of her action shocked her. Was she really having sex with Chadwick Beaumont, standing up—in front of a mirror?

Oh, hell yes, she was. And it was the hottest thing she'd ever done.

"Naughty girl," he said with a grin.

Then he began in earnest. From her angle, she couldn't see where their bodies met. She could only see his hands when he cupped her breasts to tweak a nipple or slid his fingers between her legs to stroke her center. She could only see the need on his face when he leaned forward to nip at her neck and shoulder, the raw desire in his eyes when their gazes met.

She held on to that dresser as if her life depended on it while Chadwick thrust harder and harder. "I need you so much," he called out as he grabbed her by the waist and slammed his hips into hers. "I've always needed you *so* much."

"Yes—like that," she panted, rising up to meet him each time. His words pushed her past the first orgasm. She couldn't remember ever feeling this needed, this sexual. "I'm going to—I'm—" Her next orgasm cut off her words, and all she could do was moan in pleasure.

But she didn't close her eyes. She saw how she looked

when she came—her mouth open, her eyes glazed with desire. So hot, watching the two of them together.

A roar started low in Chadwick's chest as he pumped once, twice more—then froze, his face twisted in pleasure. Then he sort of fell forward onto her, both of them panting.

"My Serena," he said, sounding spent.

"My Chadwick," she replied, knowing it was the truth.

She was his now. And he was hers.

But he wasn't. He couldn't be. He was still married. He was still her boss. One explosive sexual encounter didn't change those realities.

For tonight, he was hers.

Tomorrow, however, was going to be a problem.

Ten

Chadwick laid in Serena's bed, his eyes heavy and his body relaxed.

Serena. How long had he fantasized about bending her over the desk and taking her from behind? Years. But the mirror? Watching her watch him?

Amazing.

She came back in and shut the door behind her. Her hair was down now, hanging in long, loose waves around her shoulders. He couldn't remember ever seeing her hair down. She always wore it up. He could see her nude figure silhouetted by the faint light that trickled through her drapes. Her body did things to him—things he didn't realize he could still feel. It'd been so long....

She paused. "You need anything?"

"You." He held out his hand to her. "Come here."

She slipped into bed and curled up against his chest. "That was...wow."

Grinning, he pulled her in for a kiss. A long kiss. A kiss that involved a little more than just kissing. He could *not* get enough of her. The feeling of her filling his hands, pressed against him—she was so much a woman. He'd brought three condoms, just in case. He had the remaining two within easy reach on her bedside table.

So he broke the kiss.

"Mmmm," she hummed. "Chadwick?"

"Yes?"

She paused, tracing a small circle on his chest. "I'm pregnant."

"A fact we've already established."

"But why doesn't that bother you? I mean, everything's changing and I feel so odd and I'm going to blow up like a whale soon. I just don't think…I don't feel beautiful."

He traced a hand down her back and grabbed a handful of her bountiful backside. "You are amazingly beautiful. I guess you being pregnant just reminds me how much of a woman you are."

She was quiet for a moment. "Then why didn't you ever have kids with Helen?"

He sighed. He didn't want Helen in this room. Not now. But Serena had a right to know. Last week, they might not have discussed their personal lives at the office—but this was a different week entirely. "Did you ever meet her? Of course you did."

"At the galas. She never came by the office."

"No, she never did. She didn't like beer, didn't like my job. She only liked the money I made." Part of that was his fault. If he'd put her before the job, well, things might have been different. But they might not have been. Things might have been exactly the same.

"She was very pretty. Very—"

"Very plastic." She'd been pretty once, but with every

new procedure, she'd changed. "She had a lot of work done. Lipo, enlargements, Botox—she didn't want to have a baby because she didn't want to be pregnant. She didn't want me."

That was the hard truth of the matter. He'd convinced himself that she did—convinced himself that he wanted to spend the rest of his life with her, that it would be different from his father's marriages. That's why he'd struck the alimony clause from the pre-nup. But he'd never been able to escape the simple fact that he was Hardwick's son. All he'd ever been able to do was temper that fact by honoring his marriage vows long after there was nothing left to honor.

"She moved out of our bedroom about two years ago. Then filed for divorce almost fourteen months ago."

"That's a *very* long time." The way she said it—air rushing out of her in shock—made him hold her tighter. "Did you want to have a kid? I mean, I get her reasons, but…"

Had he ever wanted kids? It was no stretch to say he didn't know. Not having kids wasn't so much his choice as it had been the path of least resistance. "You haven't met my mother, have you?"

"No."

He chuckled. "You don't want to know her. She's—well, in retrospect, she's a lot like Helen. But that's all I knew. Screaming fights and weeks of silent treatment. And since I was my father's chosen son, she treated me much the same way she treated Hardwick. I ruined her figure, even though she got a tummy tuck. I was a constant reminder that she'd married a man she detested."

"Is that what Helen did? Scream?"

"No, no—but the silent treatment, yes. It got worse over time. I didn't want to bring a child into that. I didn't want a kid to grow up with the life I did. I didn't…I didn't want to be my father."

He couldn't help it. He took her hand and guided it around to his side—to where the skin had never healed quite right.

Serena's fingertips traced the raised scar. It wasn't that bad, he told himself. He'd been telling himself that same thing for years. Just an inch of puckered skin.

Helen had seen it, of course, and asked about it. But he hadn't been able to tell her the truth. He'd come up with some lie about a skiing accident.

"Oh, Chadwick," Serena said, in a voice that sounded like she was choking back tears.

He didn't want pity. As far as the world was concerned, he had no reason to be pitied. He was rich, good-looking and soon to be available again. Only Serena saw something else—something much more real than his public image.

He still didn't want her to feel sorry for him. So he kept talking even as she rubbed his scar. "Do you know how many half siblings I have?"

"Um, Frances and Matthew, right?"

"Frances has a twin brother, Byron. And that's just with Jeannie. My father had a third wife and had two more kids with her, Lucy and David. Johnny, Toni and Mark with his fourth wife. We know of at least two other kids, one with a nanny and one with…" He swallowed, feeling uncertain.

"His secretary?"

He winced. "Yes. There are probably more. That was why I fought against *this*," he said, pressing his lips against her forehead, "for so long. I didn't want to be him. So when Helen said she wanted to wait before we had kids—and wait and wait—I said fine. Because that's different than what Hardwick did."

Serena pulled her hand away from his scar to trace small circles on his chest again. "Those are all really good reasons. Mine were more selfish. I didn't marry Neil because my parents were married and that piece of paper didn't save them or me. I always thought we'd have kids one day, but I wanted to wait until my finances could support us. I put almost every bonus you've ever given me into savings, building up my nest egg. I thought I'd like to take some time off, but the thought of not getting that paycheck every other week scared me so much. So I waited. Until I messed up." She took a ragged breath. "And here I am."

He chewed over what she'd said. "Here with me?"

"Well...yes. Unmarried, pregnant and sleeping with my boss in clear violation of company policy." She sighed. "I've spent my adult life trying to lead a stable life. I stayed with a man I didn't passionately love because it was the safe thing to do. I've stayed in this apartment—the same place I've lived since I moved in with Neil nine years ago—because it's rent-controlled. I drive the same car I bought six years ago because it hasn't broken down. And now? This is not the most secure place in the world. It...it scares me. To be here with you."

Her whole life had been spent running away from a hellish childhood. Was that any different from his? Trying so hard to not let the sins of the father revisit the son.

Yet here he was, sleeping with his secretary. And here she was, putting her entire livelihood at risk to fall into bed with him.

No. This would not be a repeat of the past. He would not let her fall through the cracks just because he wasn't strong enough to resist her. At the very least, he hadn't gotten her pregnant and abandoned her like his father would have—even if someone else had done just that.

"I want to be here with you, even if it complicates matters. You make me feel things I didn't know I was still capable of feeling. The way you look at me...I was never a son, never really a husband. Just an employee. A bank account. When I'm with you, I feel like...like the man I was always supposed to be, but never got the chance to."

She clutched him even tighter. "You never treated me like I was an afterthought, a welfare kid. You always treated me with respect and made me feel like I could be better than my folks were. That I *was* better."

He tilted her face back. "I will *not* fail you, Serena. This complicates things, but I made you a promise. I *will* keep it."

She blinked, her eyes shining. "I know you will, Chadwick. That means everything to me." She kissed him, a tender brush that was sweeter than any other touch he'd ever felt. "I won't fail you, either."

The next kiss wasn't nearly as tender. "Serena," he groaned as she slipped her legs over his thighs, heat from her center setting his blood on fire. "I need you."

"I need you, too," she whispered, rolling onto her back. "I don't want to look at you in a mirror, Chadwick. I want to see you."

He sat back on his knees and grabbed one of the condoms. Quickly, he rolled it on and lowered himself into her waiting arms. His erection found her center and he thrust in.

She moaned as he propped himself up on one arm and filled his other hand with her breast. "Yes, just like that."

He rolled his thumb over her nipple and was rewarded when it went stiff. Her breast was warm and full and *real*.

Everything about her was real—her body, her emotions, her honesty.

Serena ran her nails down his back as she looked him in the eye, spurring him on. Over and over he plunged into her welcoming body. Over and over, waves of emotion flooded his mind.

Now that he was with her, he felt more authentic than he had in years—maybe ever. The closest he'd ever come to feeling real was the year he'd spent making beer. The brewmasters hadn't treated him with distrust, as so many people in the other departments had. They'd treated him like a regular guy.

Serena worked hard for him, but she'd never done so with the simpering air of a sycophant. Had never treated him like he was a stepping stool to bigger and better things.

This was real, too. The way her body took his in, the way he made her moan—the way he wanted to take her in his arms and never let her go....

Without closing her eyes—without breaking the contact between them—she made a high-pitched noise in the back of her throat as she tightened on his body then collapsed back against her pillow.

He drove hard as his climax roared through his ears so loudly that it blotted out everything but Serena. Her eyes, her face, her body. *Her.*

He wanted her. He always had.

This didn't change anything.

"Serena..." He wanted to tell her he loved her, but then what did that mean? Was he actually in love with her? What he felt for her was far stronger than anything he'd ever felt for another woman, but did that mean it was love?

So he bit his tongue and pulled her into his arms, burying his face into her hair.

"Stay with me," she whispered. "Tonight. In my bed."

"Yes." That was all he needed right now. Her, in his arms.

What if this was love? With Serena tucked against his chest, Chadwick started to drift off to sleep on that warm, happy thought. He and Serena. In love.

But then a horrifying idea popped into his mind, jerking him back from peaceful sleep. What if this wasn't love? What if this was mere infatuation, something that would evaporate under the harsh light of reality—reality that they might have ignored tonight but that would be unavoidable come Monday morning?

He'd slept with his assistant. Before the divorce was final.

It was exactly what his father would have done.

Eleven

The smell of crisp bacon woke him.

Chadwick rolled over to find himself alone in an unfamiliar bed. He found a clock on the side table. Half past six. He hadn't slept that late in years.

He sat up. The first thing he saw was the mirror. The one he'd watched as he made love to his assistant.

Serena.

His blood began to roar in his ears as his mind replayed the previous night. Had he really crossed that line—the one he'd sworn he would never cross?

Waking up naked in her bed, his body already aching for her, seemed to say one hell of a *yes*.

He buried his head in his hands. What had he done?

Then he heard it—the soft sound of a woman humming. It was light and, if he didn't know better, filled with joy.

He got out of bed and put his pants on. Breakfast

first. He'd think better once he had a meal in him. As he walked down the short hallway toward the kitchen, he was surprised at how sore his body was. Apparently, not having sex for a few years and then suddenly having it twice had been harder on him than running a few extra miles would have been.

He looked around Serena's place. It was quite small. There was the bedroom he'd come out of. He made another stop at the bathroom, which stood between the bedroom and another small room that was completely empty. Then he was out into the living room, which had a shabby-looking couch against one wall and a space where a flat-screen television must have been on the other. A table stood between the living room space and the kitchen. The legs and the chairs looked a bit beat up, but the table was covered by a clean, bright blue cloth and held a small, chipped vase filled with the roses he'd brought her.

His wine cellar was bigger than this apartment. The place was clearly assembled from odds and ends, but he liked it. It looked almost exactly how he'd imagined a real home would look, one in which babies might color on the walls and spill juice on the rug. One filled with laughter and joy. A place that was a *home*, not just a piece of real estate.

He found Serena standing in front of the stove, a thin blue cotton robe wrapped around her shoulders, her hair hanging in long waves down her back. Something stirred deep in his chest. Did she have anything on under the robe? She was humming as she flipped the bacon. It smelled *wonderful*.

He had a cook, of course. Even though he didn't eat at home very often, George was in charge of feeding the household staff. If Chadwick gave him enough warning, George would have something that rivaled the best restaurants in Denver waiting for him. But if Chadwick didn't, he'd eat the same thing that the maids did. Which was the norm.

He leaned against the doorway, watching Serena cook for him. This felt different than knowing that, somewhere in his huge mansion, George was making him dinner. That was George's job.

Serena frying him bacon and, by the looks of it, eggs?

This must be what people meant by "comfort food." Because there was something deeply comforting about her taking care of him. As far as he could remember, no one but a staff cook had ever made him breakfast.

Was this what normal people did? Woke up on a Sunday morning and had breakfast together?

He came up behind her and slid his arms around her waist, reveling in the way her hair smelled—almost like vanilla, but with a hint of breakfast. He kissed her neck. "Good morning."

She startled but then leaned back, the curve of her backside pressing against him. "Hi." She looked up at him.

He kissed her. "Breakfast?"

"I'm normally up before six, but I made it until a little after," she said, sounding sheepish about it.

"That's pretty early." Those were basically the same hours he kept.

"I have this boss," she went on, her tone teasing as she flipped another strip of bacon, "who keeps insane hours. You know how it is."

He chuckled against her ear. "A real bastard, huh?"

She leaned back, doing her best to look him in the eye. "Nope. I think he's amazing."

He kissed her again. This time he let his hands roam away from her waist to other parts. She pulled away and playfully smacked the hand that had been cupping her breast. "You don't want your breakfast burned, do you? The coffee's ready."

She already had a cup sitting in front of the coffee-maker. Like everything else in her place, the coffeemaker looked like it was either nine years old or something she'd bought secondhand.

She hadn't been kidding. By the looks of her apartment, she really had put every bonus in savings.

It was odd. In his world, people spent money like it was always going out of style. No one had to save because there would always be more. Like Phillip, for example. He saw a horse he wanted, and he bought it. It didn't matter how much it was or how many other horses he had. Helen had been the same, except for her it was clothing and plastic surgery. She had a completely new wardrobe every season from top designers.

Hell, he wasn't all that different. He owned more cars than he drove and a bigger house than he'd ever need, and he had three maids. The only difference was that he'd been so busy working that he hadn't had time to start collecting horses like his brother. Or mistresses, like his father. For them, everything had been disposable. Even the horses. Even the people.

Serena wasn't like that. She didn't need a new coffee-pot just because the old one was *old*. It still worked. That seemed to be good enough for her.

He filled his mug—emblazoned with the logo of a local bank—and sat at the table, watching her. She moved comfortably around her kitchen. He wasn't entirely sure where the kitchen was in his family mansion. "You make breakfast often?"

She put some bread into a late-model toaster. "I've gotten very good at cooking. It's…"

"Stable?"

"*Reassuring*," she answered with a grin. "I bring home my own bacon *and* fry it up in the pan." She brought plates with bacon and eggs to the table, and then went back for the toast and some strawberry jam. "I clip coupons and shop the sales—that saves a lot of money. Cooking is much cheaper than eating out. I think last night was the first time I'd gone out to dinner in…maybe three months?" Her face darkened. "Yes. Just about three months ago."

He remembered. Three months ago, Neil and she had "mutually" decided to end their relationship.

"Thank you for making me breakfast. I've never had someone cook for me. I mean, not someone who wasn't on staff."

She blushed. "Thank you for dinner. And the dresses. I think it's pretty obvious that I've never had anyone spend that kind of money on me before."

"You handled yourself beautifully. I'm sorry if I made you uncomfortable."

That had been his mistake. It was just that she fit in so well at the office, never once seeming out of place among the high rollers and company heads Chadwick met with. He'd assumed that was part of her world—or at least something close to it.

But it wasn't. Now that he saw her place—small, neatly kept but more "shabby" than "shabby chic"—he realized how off the mark he'd been.

She gave him a smile that was part gentle and part hot. "It was fun. But I think I'll get different shoes for next time."

Next time. The best words he'd heard in a long, long time.

They ate quickly. Mostly because he was hungry and the food was good, but also because Serena shifted in her seat and started rubbing his calf with her toes. "When do you have to leave?"

He wanted to stay at least a little bit longer. But he had things to do, even though it was Sunday—for starters, he had an interview with *Nikkei Business*, a Japanese business magazine, at two. He couldn't imagine talking about the fate of the brewery from the comfort of Serena's cozy place. How could those two worlds ever cross?

The moment the thought crossed his mind, he felt like he'd been punched in the stomach. Really, how *could* their two worlds cross? His company was imploding and his divorce was draining him dry—and that wasn't even counting the fact that Serena was pregnant. And his assistant.

He'd waited so long for Serena. She'd done admirably the night before at dinner and then the gala, but how comfortable would she really be in his world?

They still had this morning. They finished breakfast and then he tried to help her load the dishwasher. Only he kept trying to put the cups on the bottom rack, which made her giggle as she rearranged his poor attempts. "Never loaded a dishwasher before, huh?"

"What gave me away?" He couldn't bring himself to be insulted. She was right.

"Thanks for trying." She closed the dishwasher door and turned to him. "Don't worry. You're better at other things."

She put her arms around his neck and kissed him. Yeah, he didn't have to leave yet.

He stripped the robe from her shoulders, leaving it in a

heap on the floor. No, nothing underneath. Just her wonderful body. With the morning light streaming through the sheers she had hung over her windows, he could finally, fully see what he'd touched the night before.

Her breasts were large and firm. He bent down and traced her nipple with his tongue. Serena gasped as the tip went hard in his mouth, her fingers tangling through his hair. *Sensitive.* Perfect.

"Bed," she said in a voice that walked the fine line between fluttery and commanding.

"Yes, ma'am," he replied, standing back to give her a mock salute before he swept her off her feet.

"Chadwick!" Serena clutched at him, but she giggled as he carried her back down the short hall.

He laid her down on the bed, pausing only long enough to get rid of his pants. Then he was filling his hands with her breasts, her hips—covering her body with his—loving the way she touched him without abandon.

This was what he wanted—not the company, not Helen, not galas and banquets and brothers and sisters who took and took and never seemed to give back.

He wanted Serena. He wanted the kind of life where he helped cook and do the dishes instead of having an unseen staff invisibly take care of everything. He wanted the kind of life where he ate breakfast with her and then went back to bed instead of rushing off for an interview or a meeting.

He wanted to have a life outside of Beaumont Brewery. He wanted it to be with Serena.

He had no idea how to make that happen.

As he rocked into Serena's body and she clung to him, all he could think about was the way she made him feel—how he hadn't felt like this in…well, maybe ever.

This was what he wanted.

There had to be a way.

Finally, after another hour of lying in her arms, he managed to tear himself away from Serena's bed. He put on his tuxedo pants and shirt and headed for the car after a series of long kisses goodbye. How amazing did Serena look, standing in the doorway in her little robe, a coffee cup in her hand as she waved him off? It almost felt like a wife kissing her husband goodbye as he went off to work.

He was over-romanticizing things. For starters, Serena wouldn't be happy as a stay-at-home wife. It would probably leave her feeling too much like she wasn't bringing home that bacon. He knew now how very important that was to her. But they couldn't carry on like this at work. The office gossips would notice something sooner or later—and once she began to show, things would go viral in a heartbeat. He didn't want to subject her to the rumor mill.

There had to be a way. The variables ran through his mind as he drove home. He was about to lose the company. She worked for him. A relationship was against company policy. But if he lost the company...

If he lost the company, he wouldn't be her boss anymore. She might be out of a job, too, but at least they wouldn't be violating any policy.

But then what? What was next? What did he *want* to do? That was what she'd asked him. Told him, in fact. Do what he wanted.

What was that?

Make beer, he realized. That was the best time he'd had at Beaumont Brewery—the year he'd spent making beer with the brewmasters. He *liked* beer. He knew a lot about it and had played a big role in selecting the seasonal drafts for the Percheron Drafts line of craft beers. What if…

What if he sold the brewery, but kept Percheron Drafts for himself, running it as a small private business? Beaumont would be dead, but the family history of brewing would live on in Percheron Drafts. He could be rid of his father's legacy and run this new company the way he wanted to. It wouldn't be Hardwick's. It would be Chadwick's.

He could hire Serena. She knew as much about what he did as anyone. And if they formed a new company, well, they could have a different company policy.

And if they got sixty-five dollars a share for the brewery…maybe he could walk into Helen's lawyer's office and make her that offer she couldn't refuse. Everyone had a price, Matthew had said, and he was right. He quickly did the math.

If he liquidated a few extraneous possessions—cars, the jet, property, *horses*—he could make Helen an offer of $100 million to sign the papers. Even she wouldn't be able to say no to a number like that. And he'd still have enough left over to re-incorporate Percheron Drafts.

As he thought about the horses, he realized this plan would only work if he did it on his own. He would get $50 million because he actually worked for the company. But his siblings would get about $15 to $20 million each. He couldn't keep working for them. Serena had been right about that, too. If he took Percheron Drafts private, he would have to sever all financial ties with his siblings. He couldn't keep footing the bill for extravagant purchases, and what's more, he didn't want to.

The more he thought about it, the more he liked this idea. He'd be done with Beaumont Brewery—free from his father's ideas of how to run a company. Free to do things the way he wanted, to make the beer he wanted. It would be a smaller company, sure—one that wouldn't be able to pay for the big mansion or the staff or the garage full of cars he rarely drove.

He'd have to downsize his life for a while, but would that really be such a horrible thing? Serena had lived small her entire life and she seemed quite happy—except for the pregnancy thing.

He wanted to give her everything he could—but he knew she wouldn't be comfortable with extravagance. If he gave her a job in a new company, paid her a good wage, made sure she had the kind of benefits she needed...

That was almost the same thing as giving her the world. That was giving her stability.

This could work. He'd call his lawyers when he got home and run the idea past them.

This *had* to work. He had to make this happen. Because it was what he wanted.

After Serena watched Chadwick's sports car drive away, she tried not to think about what the neighbors would say about the late arrival and very late departure of such a vehicle.

But that didn't mean she didn't worry. What had she done? Besides have one of the most romantic nights in memory. A fancy dinner, glamorous gala, exquisite sex? It'd been like something out of a fairy tale, the poor little girl transformed into the belle of the ball.

How long had it been since she'd enjoyed sex that much? Things with Neil had been rote for a while. A long while, honestly. Something that they *tried* to do once a week—something that didn't last very long or feel very good.

But sex with Chadwick? Completely different. Completely *satisfying*. Even better than she'd dreamed it would be. Chadwick hadn't just done what he wanted and left it at that. He'd taken his time with her, making sure she came first—and often.

What would it be like to be with a man who always brought that level of excitement to their bed? Someone she couldn't keep her hands off—someone who thought she was sexy even though her body was getting bigger?

It would be *wonderful*.

But how was that fantasy—for that's what it was, a fantasy of epic proportions—going to become a reality? She couldn't imagine fitting into Chadwick's world, with expensive clothes and fancy dinners and galas all the time. And, as adorably hot as he'd looked standing in her kitchen in nothing but his tux trousers, she also couldn't imagine Chadwick being happy in her small apartment, clipping coupons and shopping consignment stores for a bargain.

God, how she wanted him. She'd been waiting for her chance for years, really. But she had no idea how she could bridge the gap between their lives.

In a fit of pique, Serena started cleaning. Which was saying something, as she'd already cleaned in anticipation of Chadwick possibly seeing the inside of her apartment—and her bedroom.

But there was laundry to be done, dishes to be washed, beds to be made—more than enough to keep her busy. But not enough to keep her mind off Chadwick.

She changed into her grubby sweat shorts and a stained T-shirt. What the heck was going to happen on Monday? It was going to be hard to keep her hands off him, especially behind the closed door of his office. But doing anything, even touching him, was a violation of company policy. It went against her morals to violate policies, especially ones she'd helped write.

How was she supposed to be in love with Chadwick while she worked for him?

She couldn't be. Not unless…

Unless she didn't work for him.

No. She couldn't just quit her job. Even if the whole company was about to be sold off, she couldn't walk away from a steady paycheck and benefits. The sale and changeover might take months, after all—months during which she could be covered for prenatal care, could be making plans. Or some miracle could occur and the whole sale could fall through. Then she'd be safe.

So what was she going to do about Chadwick? She didn't want to wait months before she could kiss him again, before she could hold him in her arms. She was tired of pretending she didn't have feelings for him. If things stayed the same…

Well, one thing she knew for certain was that things wouldn't stay the same. She'd slept with him—multiple times—and she was pregnant. Those two things completely changed *everything*.

She was transferring the bedsheets from the washer to the dryer when she heard something at the door. Her first thought was that maybe Chadwick had changed his mind and decided to spend the day with her.

But, as she raced for the door, it swung open. *Chadwick doesn't have a key*, she thought. And she always kept her door locked.

That was as far as she got in her thinking before Neil Moore, semi-pro golf player and ex-everything, walked in.

"Hey, babe."

"Neil?" The sight of him walking in like he'd never

walked out caused such a visceral reaction that she almost threw up. "What are you doing here?"

"Got your email," he said, putting his keys back on his hook beside the door as he closed it. He looked at her in her cleaning clothes. "You look…good. Have you put on weight?"

The boldness of this insult—for that's what it was—shook her back to herself. "For crying out loud, Neil. I sent you an email. Not an invitation to walk in, unannounced."

Another wave of nausea hit her. What if Neil had shown up two hours before—when she was still tangled up with Chadwick? Good lord. She fought the emotion down and tried to sound pissed. Which wasn't that hard, really.

"You don't live here anymore, remember? *You* moved out."

Then he said, "I missed you."

Nothing about his posture or attitude suggested this was the case. He slouched his way over to the couch—*her* couch—and slid down into it, just like he always had. What had she seen in this man, besides the stability he'd offered her?

"Is that so? I've been here for three months, Neil. Three months without a single call or text from you. Doesn't seem like you've missed me very much at all."

"Well, I did," he snapped. "I see that nothing's changed here. Same old couch, same old…" He waved his hand around in a gesture that was probably supposed to encompass the whole apartment but mostly seemed directed at her. "So what did you want to talk to me about?"

She glared at him. Maybe it would have been better if Chadwick *had* still been here. For starters, Neil would have seen that nothing was the same anymore—

she wasn't, anyway. She wasn't the same frugal executive assistant she'd been when he'd left. She was a woman who went shopping in the finest stores and made small talk with the titans of industry and looked damn good doing it. She was a woman who invited her boss into her apartment and then into her bed. She was pregnant and changing and bringing home her own bacon and frying it up in her own pan, thank you very much.

Neil didn't notice her look of death. He was staring at the spot where the TV had been before he'd taken that with him. "You haven't even gotten a new television yet? Geez, Serena. I didn't realize you were going to take me leaving so hard."

"I don't need one. I don't watch TV." A fact she would have thought he'd figured out after nine years of cohabitating—or at least figured out after she told him to take the TV when he moved. "Did you come here just to criticize me? Because I can think of a lot better ways to spend a Sunday morning."

Neil rolled his eyes, but then he sat up straighter. "You know, I've been thinking. We had nine good years together. Why did we let that get away from us?"

She could not believe the words coming out of this man's mouth. "Correct me if I'm wrong, but I believe 'we' let that get away from 'us' when you started sleeping with groupies at the country club."

"That was a mistake." He agreed far more quickly than he had when Serena had found the incriminating text messages. They'd gone out to dinner that night to try and "work things out," but it'd all fallen apart instead. "I've changed, babe. I know what I did was wrong. Let me make it up to you."

This was Neil "making it up to her"—criticizing her appearance and her apartment?

"I'll do better. Be better for you." For a second, he managed to look sincere, but it didn't last. "I heard that the brewery might get sold. You own stock in the company, right? We could get a bigger place—much nicer than this dump—and start over. It could be really good, babe."

Oh, for the love of Pete. That's what this was. He'd gotten wind of the AllBev offer and was looking for a big payout.

"What happened? Your lover go back to her husband?"

The way Neil's face turned a ruddy red answered the question for her, even though he didn't. He just went back to staring at the space where the television used to be.

The more she talked to him, the less she could figure out what she had ever seen in him. The petty little criticisms—it wasn't that those were new, it was just that she'd gotten used to not having her appearance, her housekeeping and her cooking sniped at.

In three months, she'd realized how much she'd settled by staying with Neil. No wonder the passion had long since bled out of their relationship. Hard to be passionate when the man who supposedly loved you was constantly tearing you down.

Chadwick didn't do that to her. Even before this last week had turned everything upside down, he'd always let her know how much he appreciated her hard work. That had just carried over into her bed. Boy, had he appreciated her hard work.

Serena shook her head. This wasn't exactly an either/or situation. Just because she didn't want Neil didn't necessarily mean her only other option was Chadwick. Even if whatever was going on between her and Chadwick was nothing more than a really satisfying rebound—for both of them—well, that didn't mean she wanted to throw herself at Neil. She was no longer a scared college girl existing just above the poverty line. She was a grown woman fully capable of taking care of herself.

It was a damn good thing to realize.

"I'm pregnant. You're the father." There. She'd gotten it out. "That's what I needed to talk to you about. And because *you* were sleeping around, *I* have to get tested."

For a moment, Neil was well and truly shocked. His mouth flopped open and his eyes bugged out of his head. "You're…"

"Pregnant. Have been for three months."

"Are you sure I'm the father?"

Her blood began to boil. "Of course you're the father, you idiot. Just because you were sleeping around doesn't mean I was. I was faithful to you—to *us*—until the very end. But that wasn't enough for you. And now you're not enough for me."

"I…I…" He seemed stuck.

Well, he could just stick. She was the one that was pregnant. She'd spend the rest of her life raising his—*her*—baby. But that didn't mean she had to spend the rest of her life with him. "I thought you should know."

"I didn't want—I can't—" He wasn't making a lot of progress. "Can't you just *end* it?"

"Get out." The words flew from her mouth. "Get out *now*."

"But—"

"This is my child. I don't need anything from you, and what's more is I don't *want* anything from you. I won't sue you for child support. I never want to see you again." She hadn't said that when he'd left the last time. Maybe because she hadn't believed the words. But now she did.

Neil's eyes hadn't made a lot of progress back into

his skull. "You don't want money? Damn—how much is Beaumont paying you now?"

Was that all she was—a back-up source of funding? "If you're still here in one minute, I'm calling the police. Goodbye, Neil."

He got up, looking like she'd smacked him. "Leave your key," she called after him. She didn't want any more surprise visits.

He took the key off his key ring and hung it back on the hook.

Then he closed the door on his way out.

And that was that.

She looked around the apartment as if the blinders had suddenly been lifted from her eyes. This wasn't her place. It had never been hers. This had been *their* place—hers and Neil's. She'd wanted to stay here because it was safe.

But Neil would always feel like he was entitled to be there because it had been his apartment before she'd moved in.

She didn't want to raise her baby in a place that was haunted by unfaithfulness and snide put-downs.

She needed a fresh start.

The thought terrified her.

Twelve

"Ms. Chase, if you could join me in my office."

Serena tried not to grin as she gathered up her tablet. He was paging her a full forty minutes earlier than their normal meeting time. What a difference a week made. Seven days before, she'd been shell-shocked after realizing she was pregnant. This week? She was sort of her boss's secret lover.

No, best not to think of it in those terms. Company policy and all that.

She opened the door to Chadwick's office and shut it behind her. That was what she normally did, but today the action had an air of secrecy about it.

Chadwick was sitting behind his desk, looking as normal as she'd ever seen him. Well, maybe not *that* normal. He glanced up and his face broke into one huge grin. God, he was so handsome. It almost hurt to look at him, to know that he was so happy because of her.

He didn't say anything as she walked toward her regular seat. Instead, he got up and met her halfway with the kind of kiss that melted every single part of her body. He pulled her in tight, and his lips explored hers.

"I missed you," he breathed in her ear as he wrapped his arms around her.

She took in his clean scent, her body responding to his touch. How different was this from Neil telling her he missed her the day before? Chadwick wasn't all talk. He followed up everything he said with actions.

"Me, too." Now that she knew exactly what was underneath that suit jacket, she couldn't stop running her hands over the muscles of his back. "I've never wanted Monday to get here so fast."

"Hmmm" was all he replied as he took another kiss from her. "When can I see you again?"

She gave him a look that was supposed to be stern. It must not have come across the way she intended it to, because he cracked a goofy grin. "This doesn't count?"

"You know what I mean."

She did. When could they spend another night wrapped in each other's arms? She wanted to say tonight. Right now. They could leave work and not come back until much, much later.

That wasn't an option.

"What are we going to do? I hate breaking the rules."

"You wrote the rule."

"That makes it even worse."

Instead of looking disgruntled with her, his grin turned positively wicked. "Look, I know this is a problem. But I'm working on a solution."

"Oh?"

"It's in process." She must have given him a look because he squeezed her a little tighter. "Trust me."

She stared into his eyes, wanting nothing more than to go back to Saturday night. Or even Sunday morning.

But reality was impossible to ignore. "If you need any help solving things, you just let me know."

"Done. When's your doctor's appointment?"

She touched the cleanly shaven line of his chin. "Friday next week."

"You want me to come with you?"

Love. The word floated up to the top of her consciousness, unbidden. That's what this was—love. Even if she hadn't said the exact word, she felt it with all of her heart.

Her throat closed up as tears threatened. Oh, God, she was in love with Chadwick Beaumont. It was both the best thing that had ever happened to her and one hell of a big problem.

He ran his finger under her chin again—much like he had the week before—and smiled down at her. "You all right?"

"I am. You wouldn't mind coming with me?"

"I've recently discovered that it's good to get out of the office every so often. I'd love to accompany you."

She had to swallow past the lump in her throat.

"Are you sure you're all right?"

She leaned her head against his shoulder, loving the solid, strong way he felt against her. "I hope you get that solution figured out soon."

"I won't fail you, Serena." He sounded so serious about it that she had no choice but to believe him. To hope that whatever he was planning would work. "Now, I believe I have time tonight to have a business dinner with my assistant, don't I? We can discuss my schedule in a little more...detail."

How could she say no to that? It was a business-professional activity, after all. "I believe we can make that happen."

"So," Chadwick said, pulling back and leading her toward the couch. "Tell me about your weekend."

"Funny about that." Sitting on the couch, her head against his shoulder, she related what had happened with Neil.

"You want me to take care of it?"

The way he said it—sounding much like he had when he'd nearly started a fight with his brother at the gala—made her smile. It should have been him being something of a Neanderthal male. As it was, it made her feel…secure.

"No, I think he got the message. He's not getting anything out of me or this company."

She then told Chadwick how she was thinking of moving to a new place and making a clean break with the past.

He got an odd look on his face as she talked. She knew that look—he was thinking.

"Got a solution to this problem yet?"

He cupped her face in his hands and kissed her—not the heated kiss from earlier, but something that was softer, gentler. Then he touched his forehead to hers. "You'll be the first to know."

That lump moved up in her throat again. She knew he'd keep his promise.

But what would it cost him?

"Mr. Beaumont." Serena's voice over the intercom sounded…different. Like she was being strangled.

"Yes?" He looked at Bob Larsen sitting across the desk from him, who froze mid-pitch. It wasn't like Serena to interrupt a meeting without a damn good reason.

There was a tortured pause. "Mrs. Beaumont is here to see you."

Stark panic flooded Chadwick's system. There were only a few women who went by that name and all of the options were less than pleasant. Blindly, he chose the least offensive option. "My mother?"

"Mrs. *Helen* Beaumont is here to see you."

Oh, *hell*.

Chadwick locked eyes with Bob. Sure, he and Bob had worked together for a long time, and yes, Chadwick's never-ending divorce was probably watercooler fodder, but Chadwick had worked hard to keep his personal drama and business life separate.

Until now.

"One moment," he managed to get out before he shut the intercom off. "Bob..."

"Yeah, we can pick this up later." Bob was hastily gathering his things and heading for the door. "Um... good luck?"

"Thanks." Chadwick was going to need a lot more than luck.

What was Helen doing there? She'd never come to the office when they were semi happily married. He hadn't talked to her without lawyers present in over a year. He couldn't imagine she wanted to reconcile. But what else would bring her there?

He knew one thing—he had to play this right. He could not give her something to use against him. He took a second to straighten his tie before he opened his door.

Helen Beaumont was not sitting in the waiting chairs across from Serena's desk. Instead, she was standing at one of the side windows, staring out at the brewery campus. Or maybe at nothing at all.

She was so thin he could almost see through her, like

she was a shadow instead of an actual woman. She wore a high-waisted skirt that clung to her frame, and a silk blouse topped with a fur stole. Diamonds—ones he'd paid for—covered her fingers and ears. She wasn't the same woman he'd married eight years before.

He looked at Serena, who was as white as notebook paper. Serena gave him a panicked little shrug. So she didn't have any idea what Helen was doing there, either.

"Helen." In good faith, he couldn't say it was nice to see her. So he didn't. "Shall we talk in my office?"

She pivoted on her five-inch heels and tried to kill him with a glare. "Chadwick." Her eyes cut to Serena. "I don't concern myself with what servants might hear."

Chadwick tried his best not to show a reaction. "Fine. To what do I owe the honor of a visit?"

"Don't be snide, Chadwick. It doesn't suit you." She looked down her nose at him, which was quite a feat given that she was a good eight inches shorter than he was. "My lawyer said you were going to make a new offer—the kind of offer you've refused to make for the last year."

Damn it. His lawyers were going to find themselves short one influential client for jumping the gun. Floating a trial balloon was different than telling Helen he had an offer. He hadn't even had the time to contact AllBev's negotiating team yet, for crying out loud. There was no offer until the company was sold.

He couldn't take control of his life—get the company he wanted, live the *way* he wanted—until Beaumont Brewery and AllBev reached a legally binding agreement. And what's more, none of this was going to happen overnight or even that week. Even if things moved quickly, negotiations would take months.

Plus, he hadn't told Serena about the plan to sell Beaumont but keep Percheron. God, he'd wanted to keep this all quiet until he had everything set—no more ugly surprises like this one.

"There's a difference between 'refused' and 'been unable' to make."

"Is there? Are you trying to get rid of me, Chadwick?" She managed to say it with a pout, as if he were trying to hurt her feelings.

"I've been trying to end our relationship since the month after you filed for divorce. Remember? You refused to go to marriage counseling with me. You made your position clear. You didn't want me anymore. But here we are, closing in on fourteen months later, and you insist on dragging out the proceedings."

She tilted her head to the side as she fluttered her eyelashes. "I'm not dragging anything out. I'm just...trying to get you to notice me."

"*What*? If you want to be noticed, suing a man is a piss-poor way of going about it."

Something about her face changed. For a moment he almost saw the woman who'd stood beside him in a church, making vows about love and honor.

"You *never* noticed me. Our honeymoon was only six days long because you had to get back early for a meeting. I always woke up alone because you left for the office by six every morning and then you wouldn't come back until ten or eleven at night. I guess I could have lived with that if I'd gotten to see you on the weekends, but you worked every Saturday and always had calls and interviews on Sunday. It was like...it was like being married to a ghost."

For the first time in years, Chadwick felt sympathy for Helen. She was right—he'd left her all alone in that big house with nothing to do but spend money. "But you knew this was my job when you married me."

"I—" Her voice cracked.

Was she on the verge of crying? She'd cried some, back when they would actually fight about…well, about how much he worked and how much money she spent. But it'd always been a play on his sympathies then. Was this a real emotion—or an old-fashioned attempt at manipulation?

"I thought I might be able to make you love me more than you loved this company. But I was wrong. You had no intention of ever loving me. And now I can never have those years back. I lost them to this damn brewery." She brightened, anything honest about her suddenly gone. He was looking at the woman who glared at him from across the lawyers' conference room table. "Here we are. I'm just getting what I deserve."

"We were married for less than ten years, Helen. What is it you think you deserve?"

She gave him a simpering smile and he knew the answer. *Everything.* She was going to take the one thing that had always mattered to him—the company—and she wouldn't stop until it was gone.

Until he had nothing left.

The phone rang on Serena's desk, causing him to jump. She answered it in something that sounded like her normal voice. "I'm sorry, but Mr. Beaumont is in a…meeting. Yes, I can access that information. One moment, please."

"My office," he said under his breath. "*Now.* We don't need to continue this conversation in front of Ms. Chase."

Helen's eyes narrowed until she looked like a viper mid-strike. "Oh? Or is it that you don't want to have *Ms. Chase* in front of me?"

Oh, no. He'd finally done something he wanted—taken Serena out, spent a night in her arms—and he was going to pay for it. Damn it all, why hadn't he kept his hands off her?

Because he wanted Serena. Because she wanted him.

It'd all seemed so simple two days before. But now?

"I beg your pardon," Serena said in an offended tone as she hung up the phone.

Helen's mouth twisted into a smirk. "You should. Sleeping with other people's husbands is never a good career move for a secretary."

"You can't talk to me like that," Serena said, sounding more shocked than angry.

Helen continued to stare at her, fully aware she held the upper hand in this situation. "How could you, Chadwick? Dressing up this dumpy secretary and parading her about as if she was *worth* something? I heard it was a pitiable sight."

Damn it all. He'd forgotten about Therese Hunt, Helen's best friend. Serena's face went a blotchy shade of purplish red, and she actually seemed to sway in her seat, like she might faint.

If Helen wanted his attention, she had it now. He was possessed with a crazy urge to throw himself between Serena and Helen—to protect Serena from Helen's wrath. He didn't do that, but he did take a step toward Helen, trying to draw her attention back to him.

"You will watch your mouth or I will have security escort you out of this building and, if you ever set foot on brewery property again, I'll file a restraining order so fast your head will spin. And if you think I'm not making a big enough offer now, just wait until the cops get involved. You will get nothing."

"After what you put me through, you owe me," she screeched.

Keeping his cool was turning out to be a lot of work. "I already offered you terms that are in line with what I owe you. You're the one who won't let this end. I'd like to move on with my life, Helen. Usually, when someone files for divorce, they're indicating that they, too, would like to move on with their lives—separately."

"You've been *sleeping* with her, haven't you?" Her voice was too shrill to be shouting, but loud enough to carry down the halls. Office doors opened and heads cautiously peeked out. "For how long?"

This whole situation was spiraling out of control. "Helen—"

"How long? It's been years, right? Were you banging her before we got married? *Were you*?"

Once, Helen had seemed sweet and lovely. But it had all been so long ago. The vengeful harpy before him was not the woman he had married.

It took everything he had to keep his voice calm. "I *was* faithful to you, Helen. Even after you moved out of our bedroom. But you're not my wife anymore. I don't owe you an explanation for what I do or who I love."

"The hell I'm not your wife—I haven't signed off!"

Anger roared through his body. "You are *not* my wife. You can't cling to the refuge of that technicality anymore, Helen. I've moved on with my life. For the love of God, move on with yours. My lawyers will be in contact with yours."

"You lying bastard! You stand here and take it like a man!"

"I'm not doing this, Helen. Ms. Chase, if you could join me in my office."

Serena gathered her tablet and all but sprinted through his open office door.

"You can't ignore me. I'll take everything. *Everything*!"

He positioned himself between her and the doorway to his office. "Helen, I apologize that I wasn't the man you needed me to be. I'm sorry you weren't the woman I thought you were. We both made mistakes. But move on. Take my next offer. Start dating. Find the man who *will* notice you. Because it's not me. Goodbye, Helen."

Then, over the hysterical sound of her calling him every name in the book, he shut the door.

Serena hunched in her normal chair, her head near her knees.

Chadwick picked up his phone and dialed the security office. "Len? I have a situation outside my office—I need you to make sure my ex-wife makes it out of the building as quietly as possible without you laying a hand on her. Whatever you do, *don't* provoke her. Thanks."

Then he turned his attention to Serena. Her color was not improving. "Breathe, honey."

Nothing happened. He crouched down in front of her and raised her face until he could see that her eyes were glazed over.

"Breathe," he ordered her. Then, because he couldn't think of anything else to shock her back into herself, he kissed her. Hard.

When he pulled back, her chest heaved as she sucked in air. He leaned her head against his shoulder and rubbed her back. "Good, hon. Do it again."

Serena gulped down air as he held her. What a mess. This was all his fault.

Well, his and his lawyers'. *Former* lawyers.

Outside the office, the raging stopped. Neither he nor

Serena moved until his phone rang some minutes later. Chadwick answered it. "Yes?"

"She's sitting in her car, crying. What do you want me to do?"

"Keep an eye on her. If she gets back out of the car, call the police. Otherwise, just leave her alone."

"Chadwick," Serena whispered so quietly that he almost didn't hear her.

"Yes?"

"What she said…"

"Don't think about what she said. She's just bitter that I took you to the gala." The blow about Serena being a dumpy secretary had been a low one.

"No." Serena pushed herself off his shoulder and looked him in the eye. Her color was better, but her eyes were watery. "About her being alone all the time. Because you work *all the time*."

"I did."

But that wasn't the truth, and they both knew it. He still worked that much.

She touched her fingertips to his cheek. "You *do*. I know you. I know your schedule. You left my apartment on Sunday exactly for the reason she said—because you had an interview."

All of his plans—plans that had seemed so great twenty-four hours before—felt like whispers drifting into the void.

"Things are going to change," he promised her. She didn't look like she believed him. "I'm working on it. I won't work a hundred hours a week. Because Helen was right about something else, too—I didn't love her more than I loved the company. But that's…" His voice choked up. "But that's different now. I'm different now, because of you."

Her lip trembled as two matching tears raced down either cheek. "Don't you see the impossible situation we're in? I can't be with you while I work for you—but if I don't work for you, will I ever see you?"

"Yes," he said. She flinched. It must have come out more harshly than he'd meant it to, but he was feeling desperate. "You will. I'll make it happen."

Her mouth twisted into the saddest smile he'd ever seen. "I've made your life so much harder."

"Helen did—not you. You are making it better. You always have."

She stroked his face, tears still silently dripping down her cheeks. "Everything's changed. If it were just you and me…but it's not anymore. I'm going to have a baby and I have to put that baby first. I can't live with the fear of Helen or even Neil popping up whenever they want to wreak a little havoc."

The bottom of his stomach dropped out. "I'm going to sell the company, but it'll take months. You'll be able to keep your benefits, probably until the baby's born. It doesn't have to change right now, Serena. You can stay with me."

Tears streaming, she shook her head. "I can't. You understand, don't you? I can't be your dumpy secretary and your weekend lover at the same time. I can't live that way, and I won't raise my child torn between two worlds like that. I don't belong in your world, and you—you can't fit in mine. It just won't work."

"It will," he insisted.

"And this company," she went on. "It's what you were raised to do. I can't ask you to give that up."

"Don't do this," he begged. The taste of fear was so strong in the back of his mouth that it almost choked him. "I'll take care of you, I promise."

Helen had left him, of course. But underneath the drama, he'd been relieved she was gone. It meant no more fights, no more pain. He could get on with the business of running his company without having to gauge everything against what Helen would do.

This? This meant no more seeing Serena first thing every morning and last thing every night. No more Serena encouraging him to get out of the office, reminding him that he didn't have to run the world just so his siblings could spend even more money.

The loss of Helen had barely registered on his radar. But the loss of Serena?

It would be devastating.

"I can't function without you." Even as he said it, he knew it was truer than he'd realized. "Don't leave me."

She leaned forward, pressing her wet lips to his cheek. "You can. You will. I have to take care of myself. It's the only way." She stood, letting her fingers trail off his skin. "I hereby resign my position of executive assistant, effective immediately."

Then, after a final tear-stained look that took his heart and left it lying in the middle of his office, she turned and walked out the door.

He watched her go.

So this was a broken heart.

He didn't like it.

Thirteen

The door to Lou's Diner jangled as Serena pulled it open. Things had been so crazy that she hadn't even had time to tell her mom and dad that she was pregnant. Or that she had quit her great job because she was in love with her great boss.

Mom and Dad had an old landline phone number that didn't have voice mail or even an answering machine, if it worked at all. The likelihood of her getting a "this number is out of service" message when Serena called was about fifty percent. Catching her mom at work was pretty much the only guaranteed way to talk to her parents.

She'd put off going there for a few nights. Seeing her parents always made her feel uncomfortable. She'd tried to help them out through the years—got them into that apartment, helped make the payments on her dad's car— and there'd been the disastrous experiment with prepaid cell phones. It always ended with them not being able to keep up with payments, no matter how much Serena put toward them. She was sure it had something to do with sheer, stubborn pride—they would not rely on their daughter, thank you very much. It drove Serena nuts. Why wouldn't they work a little harder to improve their situation?

Why hadn't they worked harder for her? Sure, if they wanted to be stubborn and barely scrape by, she couldn't stop them. But what about her?

Yes, she loved her parents and yes, they were always glad to see her. But she wanted better than a minimum wage job for the rest of her life, pouring coffee until the day she died because retirement was something for rich people. And what's more, she wanted better for her baby, too.

Still, there was something that felt like a homecoming, walking into Lou's Diner. Shelia Chase had worked here for the better part of thirty years, pulling whatever shift she could get. Lou had died and the diner had changed hands a few times, but her mom had always stuck with it. Serena didn't think she knew how to do anything else.

Either that, or she was afraid to try.

It'd been nine days since Serena had walked out of Chadwick's office. Nine long, anxious days that she'd tried to fill by keeping busy planning her new life.

She'd given her notice to her landlord. In two weeks, she was going to be moving into a new place out in Aurora, a good forty minutes away from the brewery. It wasn't a radically different apartment—two bedrooms, because she was sure she would need the space once the baby started crawling—but it wasn't infused with reminders of Neil. Or of Chadwick, for that matter. The rent was almost double what she was paying now, but if she bought her baby things used and continued to clip coupons, she had enough to live on for a year, maybe more.

She'd applied for ten jobs—office manager at an insurance firm, administrative assistant at a hospital, that sort of thing. She'd even sent her resume to the food bank. She knew the director had been pleased with her work and that the bank was newly flush with Beaumont cash. They could afford to pay her a modest salary—but health insurance...well, she was covered by a federal insurance extension plan. It wasn't cheap, but it would do. She couldn't go without.

She hadn't had any calls for interviews yet, but it was still early. At least, that's what she kept telling herself. Now was not the time to panic.

Except that, as she slid into a booth that was older than she was, the plastic crackling under her growing weight, the old fear of being reduced to grocery shopping in food pantries gripped her.

Breathe, she heard Chadwick say in her head. Even though she knew he wasn't here, it still felt...comforting.

Flo, another old-timer waitress with a smoker's voice, came by. "'Rena, honey, you look good," she said in a voice so gravelly it was practically a baritone. She poured Serena a cup of coffee. "Shelia's waiting on that big table. She'll be over in a bit."

So just the thought of being back in this place that had barely kept her family above water was enough to make breathing hard. There was still something comforting about the familiar—Flo and her scratchy voice, Mom waiting tables. Serena's world might have been turned completely on its ear in the last few weeks, but some things never changed.

She smiled at Flo. "Thanks. How are the grandkids?"

"Oh, just adorable," Flo said, beaming. "My daughter got a good job at Super-Mart stocking shelves, so I watch the kids at night after I get off work. They sleep like angels for me."

As Flo went to make her coffee rounds, Serena pushed back a new wave of panic. A good job stocking shelves? Having her mom watch the kids while she worked the night shift?

Yes, a job was better than no job, but this?

She'd thought that she could never be a part of Chadwick's world and he could never be a part of hers—they were just too different. But now, sitting here and watching her mother carry a huge tray of food over to a party of ten, Serena realized how much her world had really and truly changed. Once upon a time, when she was in college, a night job stocking shelves *would* have been a good job. It would have paid the rent and the grocery bills, and that was all she would have needed.

But now?

She needed more. No, she didn't need the five-thousand-dollar dresses that she hadn't been able to bring herself to pack up and return to the store. But now that she'd had a different kind of life for so long—a life that didn't exist in the spaces between paychecks—she knew she couldn't go back to one of menial labor and night shifts.

A picture of Chadwick floated before her eyes. Not the Chadwick she saw every day sitting behind his desk, his eyes glued to his computer, but the Chadwick who had stood across from her in a deserted gallery. He had been trying just as hard as she was to make things work—even if those "things" were radically different for each of them. He had been a man hanging on to his sanity by the tips of his fingers, terrified of what would happen if he let go.

In that moment, Chadwick hadn't just been a handsome or thoughtful boss. He'd been a man she understood on a fundamental level.

A man who'd understood her.

But then Helen Beaumont had come in and reminded Serena exactly how far apart her world and Chadwick's really were.

Deep down, Serena had known she couldn't carry on with Chadwick while she worked for him. An affair with her boss—no matter how passionate or torrid—wasn't who she was. But hearing how Chadwick had neglected his wife in favor of his company?

It'd been like a knife in the back. Were she and Chadwick only involved because they'd spent more time together in the past seven years than he'd ever spent with his wife—because, as Chadwick's employee, she was the only woman he spent any time with at all?

What if he was only with her because she was available? Hadn't she stayed with Neil for far too long for the exact same reason—because that was the path of least resistance?

No. She would not be the default anymore. Stability wasn't the safest route. That's what had kept her mother chained to this diner for her entire life—it was a guaranteed job. Why risk a bird in the hand when two in the bush was no sure thing?

If whatever was going on between Chadwick and Serena was more than just an affair of convenience, it would withstand her not being his executive assistant. She was sure of it.

Except for one small thing. He hadn't called. Hadn't even texted.

She hadn't really expected him to, but part of her was still disappointed. Okay, *devastated*. He'd said all those lovely things about how he was going to change, how she made him a better person—words that she had longed to hear—but actions spoke so much louder. And he hadn't done anything but watch her go.

She might love Chadwick. The odds were actually really good. But she couldn't know for sure while she worked for him. More than anything else, she didn't want to feel like he held all the cards in their relationship. She didn't want to feel like she owed everything to him—that he controlled her financial well-being.

That was why, as painful as it had been, she'd walked away from his promise to take care of her. Even though she wanted nothing more than to know that the man she loved would be there for her and that she'd never have to worry about sliding back into poverty again, she couldn't bank on that.

She was in control of her life, her fate. She had to secure her future by herself.

Serena Chase depended on no one.

Which was a surprisingly lonely way to look at the rest of her life.

Her head swimming, Serena was blinking back tears when her mother came to her table. "Sweetie, look at you! What's wrong?"

Serena smiled as best she could. Her mother was not many things, but she'd always loved her *sweetie*. Serena couldn't hide her emotional state from her mom.

"Hi, Mom. I hadn't talked to you for a while. Thought I'd drop in."

"I'm kinda busy right now. Can you sit tight until the rush clears out? Oh, I know—I'll have Willy make you some fried chicken, mashed potatoes and a chocolate shake—your favorite!"

Mom didn't cook. But she could order comfort food like a boss. "That'd be great," Serena admitted. She was eating for two now, after all. "Dad coming to get you tonight?"

That was their normal routine. If he still had a car that worked, that was.

Mom patted her on the arm. "Sure is. He got a promotion at work—he's now the head janitor! He'll be by in a few hours if you can wait that long."

"Sure can." Serena settled into the booth, enjoying the rare feeling of her mother spoiling her. She pulled out her phone and checked her email.

There was a message from Miriam Young. "Ms. Chase," it read, "I'm sorry to hear that you're no longer with the Beaumont Brewery. I'd be delighted to set up an interview. The Rocky Mountain Food Bank would be lucky to have someone with your skills on board. Call me at your earliest convenience."

Serena felt her shoulders relax. She would get another job. She'd be able to continue being her own stability.

Mom brought her a plate heaped with potatoes and chicken. "Everything okay, sweetie?"

"I think so, Mom."

Serena ate slowly. There was no rush, after all. Yes, if she could get another job lined up, that would go a long way toward being *okay*.

Yes, she'd be fine. Her and the baby. Just the two of them. Tomorrow, at her first appointment, she might get to hear the heartbeat.

The appointment Chadwick had offered to attend with her.

She knew she'd be fine on her own. She'd hardly missed Neil after a couple of weeks. It'd been a relief not to have to listen to his subtle digs, not to clean up after his messes.

Even though she'd only had Chadwick in her bed for

a night, that night had changed everything. He had been passionate and caring. He'd made her feel things she'd forgotten she needed to feel. In his arms, she felt beautiful and desirable and wanted. Very much wanted. Things she hadn't felt in so long. Things she couldn't live without.

Now that she'd tasted that sort of heat, was she really going to just do without it?

As she ate, she tried to figure out the mess that was her life. If she got a job at the food bank, then she would be able to start a relationship with Chadwick on equal footing. Well, he'd still be one of the richest men in the state and she'd still be middle class. *More* equal footing, then.

Finally, the rush settled down just as Joe Chase came through the door. "Well, look who's here! My baby girl!" he said with obvious pride as he leaned down and kissed her forehead.

Mom got him some coffee and then slid into the booth next to him. "Hey, babe," her dad said, pulling her mom into the kind of kiss that bordered on not-family-friendly.

Serena studied the tabletop. Her parents had never had money, never had true security—but they'd always had each other, for better or worse. In a small way, she was jealous of that. Even more so now that she'd glimpsed it with Chadwick.

"So," Dad said as he cleared his throat. Serena looked back at them. Dad was wearing stained coveralls and Mom looked beat from a day on her feet, but his arm was around her shoulder and she was leaning into him as if everything about the world had finally gone right.

"How's the job?"

Serena swallowed. She'd had the same job, the same apartment, for so long that she didn't know how her parents would deal with this. "Well…"

She told them how she'd decided to change jobs and

apartments. "The company may be sold," she said as both of her parents looked at her with raised eyebrows. "I'm just getting out while I can."

Her mom and dad shared a look. "This doesn't have anything to do with that boss of yours, does it?" Dad asked in a gruff voice as he leaned forward. "He didn't do nothing he shouldn't have, did he?"

"No, Dad, he's fine." She wished she could have sounded a little more convincing when she said it, because her parents shared another look.

"I don't have to work weekends now," her dad said. "I can round up a few buddies and we can get you moved in no time."

"That'd be really great," she admitted. "I'll get some beer and some pizzas—dinner for everyone."

"Nah, I got a couple of bucks in my sock drawer. I'll bring the beer."

"*Dad…*" She knew he meant it. A couple of bucks was probably all he had saved away.

Mom wasn't distracted by this argument. "But sweetie, I don't understand. I thought you liked your job and your apartment. I know it was rough on you when you were young, always moving around. Why the big change now?"

It was hard to look at them and say this out loud, so she didn't. She looked at the table. "I'm three months pregnant."

Her mom gasped loudly while her dad said, "You're *what* now?"

"Who—" was as far as her mom got.

Her dad finished the thought for her. "Your boss? If he did this to you, 'Rena, he should pay. I got half a mind to—"

"No, no. Neil is the father. Chadwick wasn't a part of

this." Or, at least, he hadn't been two weeks ago. "I've already discussed it with Neil. He has no interest in being a father, so I'm going to raise the baby by myself."

They sat there, stunned. "You—you okay doing that?" her dad said.

"We'll help out," her mom added, clearly warming to the idea. "Just think, Joe—a baby. *Flo!*" she hollered across the restaurant. "I'm gonna be a grandma!"

After that, the situation sort of became a big party. Flo came over, followed by Willy the cook and then the busboys. Her dad insisted on buying ice cream for the whole restaurant and toasting Serena.

It almost made Serena feel better. They couldn't give her material things—although her proud dad was hell-bent on trying—but her parents had always given her love in abundance.

It was nine that night before she made it back to her cluttered apartment. Boxes were scattered all over the living room.

Serena stood in the middle of it all, trying not to cry. Yes, the talk with her parents had gone well. Her dad would have all of her stuff moved in an afternoon. Her mom was already talking about layettes. Serena wasn't even sure what a layette was, but by God, Shelia Chase was going to get one. The best Serena had been able to do was to get her mom to promise she wouldn't take out another payday loan to pay for it.

Honestly, she wasn't sure she'd ever seen her parents so excited. The change in jobs and apartment hadn't even fazed them.

But the day had left her drained. Unable to deal with the mess of the living room, she went into her bedroom. That was a mistake.

There, hanging on the closet door, were the dresses. Oh, the dresses. She could hardly bear to look at the traces of finery Chadwick had lavished on her without thinking of how he'd bent her over in front of the dresser, how he'd held her all night long. How he'd promised to go with her to the doctor tomorrow. How he'd promised that he wouldn't fail her.

He was going to break his promise.

It was going to break her heart.

Fourteen

Serena got up and shaved her legs in preparation for her doctor's appointment. It seemed like the thing to do. She twisted up her hair and put on a skirt and a blouse. The formality of the outfit was comforting, somehow. It didn't make sense. But then, nothing made a lot of sense anymore.

For example, she needed to leave for the doctor's office by ten-thirty. She was dressed by eight. Which left her several hours to fret.

She was staring into her coffee cup, trying to figure out the mess in her head, when someone knocked on the door.

Neil? Surely he wouldn't have come back. She'd done a pretty thorough job of kicking him out the last time.

Maybe it was her mom, stopping in early to continue celebrating the good news. But, after another round of knocks, she was pretty sure it wasn't her mom.

Serena hurried to the door and peeked through the peephole. There, on her stoop, stood Chadwick Beaumont.

"Serena? I need to talk to you," he called, staring at the peephole.

Damn. He'd seen her shadow. She couldn't pretend she wasn't home without being totally rude.

She was debating whether or not she wanted to be *totally* rude when he added, "I didn't miss your appointment, did I?"

He hadn't forgotten. Sagging with relief, she opened the door a crack.

Chadwick was wearing a button-up shirt and trousers, with no tie or jacket. The informality looked good on him, but that might have had something to do with the grin on his face. If she didn't know better, she'd say he looked…giddy?

"I didn't think you were going to come."

He stared at her in confusion. "I told you I would." Then he looked at what she was wearing. "You already have an interview?"

"Well, yes. I quit my job. I need another one." She cleared her throat, suddenly nervous about this conversation. "I was counting on a letter of recommendation from you."

The grin on Chadwick's face broadened. It was as if all his worry from the last few years had melted away. "I should have guessed that you wouldn't be able to take time off. But you can cancel your interview. I found a job for you."

"You *what*?"

"Can I come in?"

She studied him. He'd found her a job? He'd come for her appointment? What was going on? Other than him being everything she'd hoped he'd be for the last week and a half. "It's been ten days, you know. Ten days without so much as a text from you. I thought…"

He stepped into the doorway—not pushing her aside, but cupping her face with his hand and stroking her chin with his fingertips. She shuddered into his touch, stunned by how much it affected her. "I was busy."

"Of course. You have a business to run. I know that."

That's why Serena walked out. She needed to see if he would still have feelings for her if she wasn't sitting outside his office door every day.

"Serena," he said, his voice deep with amusement. "Please let me come in. I can explain."

"I understand, Chadwick. I really do." She took a deep breath, willing herself not to cry. "Thank you for remembering the appointment, but maybe it's best if I go by myself."

He notched up an eyebrow as if she'd thrown down the gauntlet. "Ten minutes. That's all I'm asking. If you still think we need some time apart after that, I'll go. But I'm not walking away from you—from what we have."

Then, just because he apparently could, he stroked his fingers against her chin again.

The need to kiss him, to fall back into his arms, was almost overpowering. But that emotion was in a full-out war with her sense of self-preservation.

"What did we have?"

The grin he aimed at her made her knees suddenly shake. He leaned in, his cheek rubbing against hers, and whispered in her ear, "*Everything.*"

Then he slipped a hand around her waist and pulled her into his chest. His lips touched the space underneath her ear, sending heat rushing from her neck down her back and farther south.

God, how she wanted this. Why had she thought she could walk away from him? From the way he made her feel? "Ten minutes," she heard herself murmur as she managed to push him far enough back that she could step to the side and let him in.

So she could stop touching him.

Chadwick walked into her apartment and looked around. "You're already moving?"

"Yes. This was where I lived with Neil. I need a fresh start. All the way around," she added, trying to remember why. Oh, yes. Because she couldn't fall for Chadwick while she worked for him. And work was all he did.

She expected him to say something else, but instead he gave her a look she couldn't quite read. Was he... amused? She didn't remember making a joke.

As he stood in the middle of the living room, she saw for the first time that he was holding a tablet. "I had this plan." He began tapping the screen. "But Helen forced my hand. So instead of doing this over a couple of months, I had to work around the clock for the last ten days."

If this was him convincing her that he'd find a way to see her outside of work, he was doing a surprisingly poor job of it. "Is that so?"

He apparently found what he was looking for because he grinned up at her and handed her the tablet. "It won't be final until the board votes to accept it and the lawyers get done with it, but I sold the company."

"You *what*?" She snatched the tablet out of his hands and looked at the document.

Letter of intent, the header announced underneath the insignia of the brewery's law firm. *AllBev hereby agrees to pay $62 a share for The Beaumont Brewery and all related Beaumont Brewery brands, excluding Perche-ron Drafts. Chadwick Beaumont reserves the right to* *keep the Percheron Drafts brand name and all related recipes....*

The whole thing got bogged down in legalese after that. Serena kept rereading the first few lines. "Wait, what? You're keeping Percheron?"

"I had this crazy idea," he said, taking the tablet back from her and swiping some more. "After someone told me to do what I wanted—for me and no one else—I remembered how much I liked to actually make beer. I thought I might keep Percheron Drafts and go into business for myself, not for the Beaumont name. Here." He handed her back the tablet again.

She looked down at a different lawyer's letter—this one from a divorce attorney. *Pursuant to the case of Beaumont v. Beaumont, Mrs. Helen Beaumont (hereby known as Plaintiff) has agreed to the offer of Mr. Chadwick Beaumont (hereby known as Defendant) for alimony payments in the form of $100 million dollars. Defendant will produce such funds no later than six months after the date of this letter....*

Serena blinked at the tablet. The whole thing was shaking—because she was shaking. "I...I don't understand."

"Well, I sold the brewery and I'm using the money I got for it to make my ex-wife an offer she can't refuse. I'm keeping Percheron Drafts and going into business myself." He took the tablet from her and set it down on a nearby box. "Simple, really."

"*Simple?*"

He had the nerve to nod as if this were all no big deal—just the multi-billion dollar sale of an international company. Just paying his ex-wife $100 million.

"Serena, breathe," he said, stepping up and wrapping his arms around her. "Breathe, babe."

"What did you do?" she asked, unable to stop herself from leaning her head against his warm, broad chest. It was everything she wanted. He was everything she wanted.

"I did something I should have done years ago—I stopped working for Hardwick Beaumont." He leaned her back and pressed his lips against her forehead. She felt herself breathe in response to his tender touch. "I'm free of him, Serena. Well and truly free. I don't have to live my life according to what he wanted, or make choices solely because they're the opposite of what he would have done. I can do whatever I want. And what I want is to make beer during the day and come home to a woman who speaks her mind and pushes me to be a better man and is going to be a great mother. A woman who loves me not because I'm a Beaumont, but in spite of it."

She looked up at him, aware that tears were trickling down her cheeks but completely unable to do anything about it. "This is what you've been doing for the last ten days?"

He grinned and wiped a tear off her face. "If I could have finalized the sale, I would have. It'll still take a few months for all the dust to settle, but Harper should be happy he got his money *and* got even with Hardwick, so I don't think he'll hold up the process much."

"And Helen? The divorce?"

"My lawyers are working to get a court date next week. Week after at the latest." He gave her a look of pure wickedness. "I made it clear that I couldn't wait."

"But...but you said a job? For me?"

His arms tightened around her waist, pulling her into his chest like he wasn't ever going to let her go. "Well, I'm starting this new business, you see. I'm going to need someone working with me who can run the offices, hire the people—a partner, if you will, to keep things going while I make the beer. Someone who understands how I operate. Someone who's not afraid of hard work. Someone who can pick a good health care plan and organize a party and understand spreadsheets." He rubbed her back as he started rocking from side to side. "I happen to know the perfect woman. She comes very highly recommended. Great letter of reference."

"But I can't be with you while I work for you. It's against company policy!"

At that, he laughed. "First off—new company, new policies. Second off, I'm not hiring you to be my underling. I'm asking you to be my partner in the business." He paused then and cleared his throat. "I'm asking you to marry me."

"You *are*?"

"I am." He dropped to his knees so suddenly that she almost toppled forward. "Serena Chase, would you marry me?"

Her hand fluttered over her stomach. "The baby…"

He leaned forward and kissed the spot right over her belly button. "I want to adopt this baby, just as soon as your old boyfriend severs his parental rights."

"What if he won't?" She was aware the odds of that were small—Neil had shown no interest in being a father. But she wasn't going to just throw herself into Chadwick's arms and believe that love would solve all the problems in the world.

Even if it felt like that were true right now.

Chadwick looked up at her, his scary businessman face on. "Don't worry. I can be *very* persuasive. Be my wife, Serena. Be my family."

Could they do that? Could she work with him, not *for* him? Could they be partners *and* a family?

Could she trust that he'd love her more than he loved his company?

He must have sensed her worry. "You told me to do what makes me happy," he told her as he stood again, folding her back into his arms. "*You* make me happy, Serena."

"But...where will we live? I don't want to live in that big mansion." The Beaumont Estate was crawling with too many ghosts—both dead and living.

He smiled down at her. "Anywhere you want."

"I...I already signed a lease for an apartment in Aurora."

He notched an eyebrow at her. "We can live there if you really want. Or you can break the lease. I'll have enough left from my golden parachute that we won't have to worry about money for a long, long time. And I promise not to drop thousands on gowns or jewels for you anymore. Except for this one."

He reached into his pocket and pulled out a small dark blue box. It was just the right size for a ring.

As he opened it, he said, "Would you marry me, Serena? Would you make me a happy man for the rest of my life and give me the chance to do the same for you? I won't fail you, I promise. You are the most important person in my life and you will always come first."

Serena stared at the ring. The solitaire diamond was large without being ostentatious. It was perfect, really.

"Well," she replied, taking the box from him. "Maybe a gown every now and then...."

Chadwick laughed and swept her into his arms. "Is that a yes?"

He was everything she wanted—passion and love and stability. He wouldn't fail her.

"*Yes.*"

He kissed her then—a long, hard kiss that called to mind a certain evening in front of a mirror. "Good," he said.

It was.

* * * * *

THE BEAUMONT HEIRS *trilogy continues with*

TEMPTED BY A COWBOY
Available October 2014

A BEAUMONT CHRISTMAS WEDDING
Available November 2014

Coming soon from Sarah M. Anderson
and Harlequin Desire!

COMING NEXT MONTH FROM

HARLEQUIN

Desire

Available October 7, 2014

#2329 STRANDED WITH THE RANCHER
Texas Cattleman's Club: After the Storm • by Janice Maynard
Feuding neighbors Beth and Drew must take shelter from a devastating tornado. Trapped by the wreckage, they give in to an attraction that's been simmering for months. Can they find common ground after the storm settles?

#2330 THE CHILD THEY DIDN'T EXPECT
Billionaires and Babies • by Yvonne Lindsay
After one amazing night, Alison is shocked to learn her lover is her new client—and he's assumed guardianship of his orphaned nephew. Soon, she wants this family as her own—but can she stay once she learns the truth about the baby?

#2331 FOR HER SON'S SAKE
Baby Business • by Katherine Garbera
Driven by family rivalry, Kell takes over single mom Emma's company. But carrying out his plan means another son will grow up seeking revenge. Is Kell brave enough to fight *for* Emma, instead of against her, and change his legacy?

#2332 HER SECRET HUSBAND
Secrets of Eden • by Andrea Laurence
When Julianne and Heath come home to help their family, they're forced to face their past, including their secret nuptials. As passion brings them together a second time, will a hidden truth ruin their chance at happiness again?

#2333 TEMPTED BY A COWBOY
The Beaumont Heirs • by Sarah M. Anderson
Rebellious cowboy Phillip Beaumont meets his match in horse trainer Jo Spears. He's never had to chase a woman, but the quiet beauty won't let him close—which only makes him more determined to tempt her into his bed....

#2334 A HIGH STAKES SEDUCTION • by Jennifer Lewis
While the straight-laced Constance investigates the books at John Fairweather's casino, she's secretly thrilled by the mysterious owner's seduction. But the numbers don't lie. Can she trust the longing in his eyes, or is he playing another game?

YOU CAN FIND MORE INFORMATION ON UPCOMING HARLEQUIN® TITLES, FREE EXCERPTS AND MORE AT WWW.HARLEQUIN.COM.

REQUEST YOUR FREE BOOKS!
2 FREE NOVELS PLUS 2 FREE GIFTS!

HARLEQUIN® *Desire*

ALWAYS POWERFUL, PASSIONATE AND PROVOCATIVE

YES! Please send me 2 FREE Harlequin Desire® novels and my 2 FREE gifts (gifts are worth about $10). After receiving them, if I don't wish to receive any more books, I can return the shipping statement marked "cancel." If I don't cancel, I will receive 6 brand-new novels every month and be billed just $4.55 per book in the U.S. or $4.99 per book in Canada. That's a savings of at least 13% off the cover price! It's quite a bargain! Shipping and handling is just 50¢ per book in the U.S. and 75¢ per book in Canada.* I understand that accepting the 2 free books and gifts places me under no obligation to buy anything. I can always return a shipment and cancel at any time. Even if I never buy another book, the two free books and gifts are mine to keep forever.

225/326 HDN F4ZC

Name _____ (PLEASE PRINT)

Address _____ Apt. #

City _____ State/Prov. _____ Zip/Postal Code

Signature (if under 18, a parent or guardian must sign)

Mail to the **Harlequin® Reader Service:**
IN U.S.A.: P.O. Box 1867, Buffalo, NY 14240-1867
IN CANADA: P.O. Box 609, Fort Erie, Ontario L2A 5X3

Want to try two free books from another line?
Call 1-800-873-8635 or visit www.ReaderService.com.

* Terms and prices subject to change without notice. Prices do not include applicable taxes. Sales tax applicable in N.Y. Canadian residents will be charged applicable taxes. Offer not valid in Quebec. This offer is limited to one order per household. Not valid for current subscribers to Harlequin Desire books. All orders subject to credit approval. Credit or debit balances in a customer's account(s) may be offset by any other outstanding balance owed by or to the customer. Please allow 4 to 6 weeks for delivery. Offer available while quantities last.

Your Privacy—The Harlequin® Reader Service is committed to protecting your privacy. Our Privacy Policy is available online at www.ReaderService.com or upon request from the Harlequin Reader Service.

We make a portion of our mailing list available to reputable third parties that offer products we believe may interest you. If you prefer that we not exchange your name with third parties, or if you wish to clarify or modify your communication preferences, please visit us at www.ReaderService.com/consumerschoice or write to us at Harlequin Reader Service Preference Service, P.O. Box 9062, Buffalo, NY 14269. Include your complete name and address.

HD13R

SPECIAL EXCERPT FROM

 HARLEQUIN®

 Desire

*Read on for a sneak preview
of* USA TODAY *bestselling author*
Janice Maynard's
STRANDED WITH THE RANCHER,
the debut novel in
**TEXAS CATTLEMAN'S CLUB:
AFTER THE STORM.**
Trapped in a storm cellar after the worst tornado to hit
Royal, Texas, in decades, two longtime enemies need
each other to survive…

Beth stood and went to the ladder, peering up at their prison door. "I don't hear anything at all," she said. "What if we have to spend the night here? I don't want to sleep on the concrete floor. And I'm hungry, dammit."

Drew heard the moment she cracked. Jumping to his feet, he took her in his arms and shushed her. He let her cry it out, surmising that the tears were healthy. This afternoon had been scary as hell, and to make things worse, they had no clue if help was on the way and no means of communication.

Beth felt good in his arms. Though he usually had the urge to argue with her, this was better. Her hair was silky, the natural curls alive and bouncing with vitality. Though he had felt the pull of sexual attraction between them before, he had never acted on it. Now, trapped in the dark with nothing to do, he wondered what would happen if he kissed her.

Wondering led to fantasizing, which led to action.

HDEXP0914

Tangling his fingers in the hair at her nape, he tugged back her head and looked at her, wishing he could see her expression. "Better now?" The crying was over except for the occasional hitching breath.

"Yes." He felt her nod.

"I want to kiss you, Beth. But you can say no."

She lifted her shoulders and let them fall. "You saved my life. I suppose a kiss is in order."

He frowned. "We saved *each other's* lives," he said firmly. "I'm not interested in kisses as legal tender."

"Oh, just do it," she said, the words sharp instead of romantic. "We've both thought about this over the last two years. Don't deny it."

He brushed the pad of his thumb over her lower lip. "I wasn't planning to."

When their lips touched, something spectacular happened. Time stood still. Not as it had in the frantic fury of the storm, but with a hushed anticipation.

Don't miss the first installment of the

TEXAS CATTLEMAN'S CLUB: AFTER THE STORM *miniseries,*

STRANDED WITH THE RANCHER

by USA TODAY *bestselling author*

Janice Maynard.

Available October 2014 wherever Harlequin® Desire books and ebooks are sold.

HARLEQUIN®

Desire

POWERFUL HEROES... SCANDALOUS SECRETS... BURNING DESIRES!

THE CHILD THEY DIDN'T EXPECT

by *USA TODAY* bestselling author

Yvonne Lindsay

Available October 2014

Surprise—it's a baby!

After their steamy vacation fling, Alison Carter knows
Ronin Marshall is a skilled lover and a billionaire businessman.
But a *father*...who hires her New Zealand baby-planning service?
This divorcée has already been deceived once;
Ronin's now the last man she wants to see.

But he must have Ali. Only she can rescue Ronin from the upheaval
of caring for his orphaned nephew...and give Ronin more of what
he shared with her during the best night of his life. But something is
holding her back. And Ronin will stop at nothing to find out what
secrets she's keeping!

This exciting new story is part of the Harlequin® Desire's
popular *Billionaires & Babies* collection featuring
powerful men...wrapped around their babies' little fingers!

Available wherever books and ebooks are sold.

Talk to us online!
www.Facebook.com/HarlequinBooks
www.Pinterest.com/HarlequinBooks
www.Twitter.com/HarlequinBooks

HD73343

6715

HARLEQUIN®

Desire

POWERFUL HEROES... SCANDALOUS SECRETS... BURNING DESIRES!

Come explore the *Secrets of Eden*—where keeping the past
buried isn't so easy when love is on the line!

HER SECRET HUSBAND
by Andrea Laurence

Available October 2014

Love, honor—and vow to keep the marriage a secret!

Years ago, Heath Langston eloped with Julianne Eden.
Their parents wouldn't have approved. So when the marriage
remained unconsummated, they went their separate ways without
telling anyone what they'd done.

Now family turmoil forces Heath and Julianne back into the same
town—into the same house. Heath has had enough of living a lie.
It's time for Julianne to give him the divorce she's avoided for so long—or
fulfill the promise in her smoldering glances and finally become his wife
in more than name only.

Other scandalous titles from Andrea Laurence's
Secrets of Eden:

UNDENIABLE DEMANDS
A BEAUTY UNCOVERED
HEIR TO SCANDAL

Available wherever books and ebooks are sold.

HD73345